WARNING
YOU HAVE BEEN FOREWARNED!

This is not a romance. It will register as an emotional breach before your mind forms resistance. Clarity arrives first as your body answers with a compression behind your chest.

Once your breath shortens without permission... your muscles brace before meaning appears. Now that recognition does not ask... it arrives intact and settles where your defenses cannot reach. Gently... it comes like being seen by something that has always known you.

Reality becomes familiar without safety and intimate without comfort. Understanding it is accurate without mercy and precise without explanation. Everything felt... yes... it does not fade.

Now it embeds itself in your breathing... yes... in your body and waits. Coming forward... this novel does not soothe or heal. Everything it offers does not promise peace or refuge.

Stopping intensifies the internal pressure... while proceeding regulates it. Relief exists only in forward motion and never in retreat. A truth you sensed long ago steps closer into your body.

It is the truth you have learned to manage rather than face. You named it strength and discipline and adulthood. You felt it harden behind your chest each year it remained unspoken.

You are entering the story of a man who sees what you hide without approaching it. He does not chase... persuade or seduce. He waits because your nervous system will move you closer before your mind decides.

You are also entering the story of a woman who survived by containment and learned to call numbness calm. Once recognition begins... yes... control collapses. This story does not stay on the page.

It occupies the space behind your chest where breath learned to stay shallow. It remains present when you attempt to leave because awareness... once activated... does not reverse. This is the door and it stands open for you... yes... now.

You are being dared to step through it. Enter this story... *The Rare Flower*... or turn away. Either response... yes... you will be forever changed.

YOU HAVE BEEN FOREWARNED!

THE
RARE FLOWER

PETER J. MERRICK

THE RARE FLOWER
Copyright 2026 by Peter J. Merrick

ISBN: 979-8-9944743-2-7 eBook
ISBN: 979-8-9944743-0-3 Paperback
ISBN: 979-8-9944743-1-0 Hardcover

CHAPTER ONE

Queen of the Night

Seven-year-old Johnny walked through the park with quiet steps... a small boy carrying a presence far older than his years. His hair caught the soft morning light and his sun-touched skin held the warmth of long days outdoors. Clarity lived in his eyes which held something deeper than childhood... moving as if he was already shaping the space around him with his awareness.

Once he moved... a calm and grounded certainty radiated from him that did not belong to boys his age. Now he did not shrink to match the noise of the playground but simply moved through it with steadiness. Guided by the sense of his place in the world... he walked as if no one else could name the truth he carried.

Reality meant he understood their games and knew the rules of how to join and how to win. Underneath it all... the thought of winning felt empty... a hollow pursuit that evaporated the moment he touched it. Everything inside him pulled toward depth and meaning and stillness... yes... always forward beyond the surface of things.

Now nothing in the playground reached him because he longed for recognition that came from inside the eyes of another. Coming toward him was the sacred moment when one soul turns toward another and silently says I see you. Everything sensitive... introspective... and gentle was what he adored as his longing felt ancient even at seven.

He was yearning for someone who lived in the hidden layers of the world and would not flinch when she found him there. He could not name this desire... yet it guided every step he took as naturally as breath. Then he saw her.

She sat beneath the deep shade of an oak... a quiet island in the storm of noise around her. She held herself with stillness that did not ask to be noticed... yet radiated a presence stronger than the entire playground. Her posture was soft and protective of something sacred within her.

Without asking permission... he seemed to move on a softer frequency untouched by the chaos. The moment Johnny's awareness moved toward her something shifted inside her. In her hands she held a single flower.

It was a bloom impossibly rare for a playground and a symbol rather than a decoration. She held it with reverence as if it was a secret she still feared exposing. The way she cradled it revealed the quiet tenderness she lived inside.

This was a tenderness she did not believe anyone else would understand. Johnny stopped walking. His breath rose in a slow firm pull through his chest.

Recognition moved through him like a deep wave rising from somewhere hidden... a wave older than either of them. She was separate the way he was separate. She felt the world rather than merely seeing it.

His awareness reached toward her and she felt it land... yes. It was a subtle meeting that neither of them could explain. The other children would see a weed and they would crush it or toss it aside.

Johnny saw its deeper meaning and the offering in her hands. He saw her longing to be understood through symbols rather than words. He knew the language she spoke without ever speaking.

He stepped toward her... led by a movement that rose inside

him like instinct. Nothing in him needed to hide as he walked with intention. Quiet Storm received his approach with the sensitivity she hid from everyone else.

Her breath drew higher beneath her ribs as his presence moved closer. He recognized the bloom as the Queen of the Night. This rare black tulip lived only under perfect conditions and the right hands.

It asked for patience and protection... yes... the same qualities Johnny naturally carried. Someone called his name across the playground... yet the sound dissolved before reaching him. Johnny crossed the grass with soft deliberate steps.

A boy moved toward a destiny that called him in a voice only he could hear. Little Johnny was in search of his rare flower beneath the Quiet Storm. Anything else was unacceptable because he was in search of his audience of one.

"Hi..." he whispered... voice firm and gentle. It was the voice of someone entering truth rather than conversation. She looked up.

Her eyes widened as something deep inside her reacted before she had the chance to resist. Warmth surged throughout her spine and an opening she had never felt rose through her small body. For a moment she truly saw him.

It felt like standing at the threshold of a story she had been waiting for. It felt like home wrapped in the shape of a stranger... yes. She had been leaning against this doorway her entire little life.

Johnny pointed softly to the flower she held. "That is the Queen of the Night... the rarest black tulip in the world." He told her it only survives when the world gives it exactly what it needs.

Her body already knew and her breath trembled. He did not see a flower... he saw her symbolism and her longing. He knew the quiet offering she carried in her hands.

No one had ever spoken to the part of her that lived beneath words. Warmth gathered in her... yes... a rising sensation that frightened her because it felt too familiar. Then Johnny leaned in slightly.

His curiosity sharpened and his mind moved forward with natural masculine momentum. He asked how it stays alive after being picked and if it needs special water. He wanted to see the stem and understand how it survives.

The shift hit her like a sudden change in temperature. His eagerness felt too close and too inside. His movement pressed against her inner world before she had even decided if she felt safe.

She needed gentle pacing and time to breathe. His curiosity felt like someone stepping into the deepest room of her heart without knocking. Fear rose.

She feared being seen and then found unworthy or having the magic disappear. She feared losing something precious by exposing it. Her shield rose fast and instinctive... yes.

It was the same shield that had saved her from countless disappointments. "It is okay..." she murmured... withdrawing into herself. "I have to go soon..."

She turned inward into the safety she trusted more than hope. Johnny felt the wall appear and the dimming of something bright. He felt the ache of possibility collapsing.

Johnny **rubbed his forearm** with a slow... grounded motion. He stepped back... giving her the space she needed. He was honoring her pace even though he wished the moment had lasted longer.

Between them rested the Queen of the Night. It was a symbol of everything rare and waiting for the right season to bloom. Then Quiet Storm... an adult... yes... now grown up... jolted awake as the alarm shattered the dream.

Her heart pounded and her breath pulled sharply up into her chest... yes. Now... then... now... then... Again and again.

She sat upright in the grey hush of morning and worked to return to her body. She worked to firm the trembling behind her chest and anchor herself back into the room. The bed and the walls all felt real again... yet altered.

It was as though something from the dream had crossed the threshold beside her bed. She felt a shift moving toward her life... a quiet signal rising from a place beyond thought. The morning air felt alive and humming softly.

She let her hand press gently into the blanket as if anchoring herself to the world. Her favorite book lay open beside her where she had fallen asleep reading. It was the author whose words always reached the quietest part of her... yes.

She placed her hand across the open page and felt a trembling that deepened. A soft warmth gathered along the tender inner line of her thighs. Heat rose through her body with a quiet inevitability.

Her body already knew it was not fear but something approaching. The morning felt like the beginning of a story foreshadowed. It was the one she had been waiting her entire life to enter.

A story was already awakening inside her. What she did not know then was that this moment did not belong to sleep or memory. It did not dissolve with daylight.

It remained carried quietly beneath her days and shaping what she noticed. She could never fully forget. Yes... the Queen of the Night had already been named once.

What is named that early in the language of the unconscious does not loosen its hold. It waits patiently until life grows quiet enough to hear it again. It was something placed quietly beneath waking life where thought does not reach first.

What is named that early does not ask to be recalled. It waits... adjusting breath and posture and orientation. It waits until the world slows enough to feel it again... yes... permanently.

Something rare had been recognized and then released. That recognition did not dissolve but settled deep. It was like a seed pressed into soil long before the season arrives.

As the stillness settled over her... Quiet Storm placed her **hand over her heart**. She felt the pulse of the story beginning. Then... she chose to **detach** from the lingering dream and move into the day.

CHAPTER TWO

The Day The City
Held Its Breath

Johnny Meadows arrived in Manhattan on a morning that felt suspended between seasons... a morning he claimed with quiet authority. Clarity lived in the air which tasted like a memory he had not lived yet... yes... a memory reaching toward him as if answering his presence. Once he stepped out of the yellow taxi... he moved with the calm assurance of a man who no longer needed the world to decide his worth.

Now his life in San Diego had given him a peace he had forged through fire after the near-death experience that stripped every illusion. Grounded by the choice he made while staring at the thin line between this world and the beyond... he walked into New York City with firm presence. Reality was something he moved rather than waited for... yes... aligned with a destiny he chose to meet without hesitation.

Underneath the city's usual impatience... he allowed none of the horns or rushed footsteps to touch his internal center. Every movement shaped the environment rather than reacting to it... carrying the grounded serenity of a Stoic shaped by decades of intense living. Now... though his storied career and textbooks still sat in MBA programs across North America... none of those accomplishments defined him.

Completely carved by the near-death experience... he left behind the noise and distraction to command only purpose from within his environment. Every step through the city carried that quiet command as the world responded to his direction and not the other way around. He paused at the crosswalk and let his gaze travel along the street.

People streamed past him... eyes fixed on screens and destinations and small urgent storms that did not matter. Johnny stood in the middle of it all with the ease of a man who had stepped outside the trance. He felt something subtle underneath the concrete and glass... a current... a pull.

New York City had its own nervous system... and on this morning... yes... the city felt as if it held its breath for him. Yes... it settled. Johnny stepped inside the bookstore and breathed in the soft scent of paper and ink.

He was claiming a sanctuary he had long forgotten he deserved. The shift from street to shelves felt like entering another layer of reality. It felt like stepping into a space that answered something in him he had not named... yes.

This was a room that recognized him. Johnny moved through the aisles with quiet appreciation and awe. He let his fingers drift gently along the spines of books that had shaped others.

He wished to feel their journeys rise beneath his touch. Without asking permission... he then paused in front of a display table. He noticed a copy of his earlier work resting between two contemporary novels.

The placement looked accidental... yet his presence made it feel intentional... as if the book had been waiting for him. His reflection glanced back from the glossy cover. He took in the man he had become... not with pride... rather with a grounded acceptance.

This was an acknowledgment that he had earned his own respect through the University of Hard Knocks. He had survived it. He lifted the book from the display and opened it to a random page.

It was as if he were claiming a moment with his former self. His eyes slid over the sentences he had written years before. They were shaped by a younger version of himself who had not yet walked through the ultimate fire.

He now regarded that version with a quiet understanding and appreciation. It revealed how far he had traveled inside his own life. His present self acted upon the past... not the other way around.

He chose which memories had the right to be remembered and would be permitted to speak. There was a distance between the writer he had been and the writer he had become. Yet both carried the same center and the same longing for deeper meaning.

The same impulse lived in him to offer something real to anyone willing to feel. This was something that rose from a place he no longer resisted and no longer apologized for. He closed the book gently and set it down.

The movement was deliberate... controlled... and masculine in its certainty. It was as if he were placing a full stop at the end of an old chapter. Then he felt it... yes.

There was a subtle shift in the atmosphere behind him. It was like the faint stirring of a breeze in a sealed room he had just claimed. He did not turn immediately.

He allowed the moment to breathe... choosing to let the feeling come to him. He was trusting the instinct that had saved him countless times in life. A presence had entered the sacred sanctuary of the bookstore.

It was not loud or disruptive... but it carried an unmistakable depth that responded to his field. Something in the room leaned toward that presence... and something in him leaned back. When Johnny finally turned... his awareness moved first.

Then his gaze landed on her... Quiet Storm. His gaze claimed the moment before she even understood she had created it. Her posture was elegant and her presence softened by an inner pain.

This pain both quenched her soul and stirred a quiet longing. It was a tension she tried to conceal behind her sophisticated shield of grace. Her body remembered.

She stood as if the world had asked too much of her for too long. Yet she still refused to harden. Her fingers rested on a copy of *The Rare Flower* as if the book itself had reached for her... yes.

It was as if his words had selected her from the inside out. The sight landed in his chest with a weight that surprised him. For the first time in a long time... Johnny recognized a movement he chose not to interrupt.

It was recognition... yes. It was a familiar knowing he could not place. He felt it settle low and firm... the kind of recognition that tells a man his life is about to tilt.

He held his attention on her for a breath longer... simply with presence. He let his attention rest on her without reaching for her. He was aware that even his noticing carried weight.

She received the force of his presence without looking up yet. It moved deep in her core and traveled through her skin. It was as if her body registered him before her conscious mind was willing to admit it.

Johnny allowed the moment to unfold without interference. Her body already knew. He knew real encounters happened when two inner worlds stopped pretending at the same time.

Quiet Storm had come to the bookstore for refuge... not revelation. Her morning had been efficient and externally controlled. This was exactly the way she believed her life needed to be to hold herself together.

Contracts and emails and quiet negotiations had pressed the

rawness behind her chest into stillness. She was wrapping herself in a false competence and belief she was in control. She had dressed herself into a protective shell that looked like elegance.

Then she stepped into the city with the poise of a woman who pretended to carry responsibility. She did this without complaint or feminine longings. By the time she reached the bookstore... her mind needed quiet retreat.

She needed inner stillness more than it needed answers. She drifted through the aisles with the familiar grace of a woman shaped by words. This was more deeply than anyone would ever suspect.

The books did not demand explanations or justifications. They simply reached for the part of her that hid behind her fake composure... yes. This was especially the part she kept hidden from the world and even from herself.

She moved past rows of book titles until one display stopped her. It was as if it had placed itself in her path. The Rare Flower.

Her hand moved before thought could interfere. She lifted the book gently... the way a woman lifts something forbidden. It was something that had already entered her dreams and her desires... yes.

It had entered into her body. These were deep... lost secrets... yes. They ignited her most feminine hidden hungers and the tender ache beneath them.

Her fingertips traced the title... then his name... Johnny Meadows. She had whispered that name into the dark more than once. It was like a confession that never reached another human ear.

She allowed his syllables to rest against her lips. Johnny Meadows' words had moved through her many times... more than she could count... yes. They moved with a sensual pulse that awakened her skin and her spine.

They awakened her inner most longings and her inner thighs. Johnny Meadows had given her a sensual language she did not have before him. Her throat tightened in the familiar way.

Her body recognized the mirror before her mind allowed this

admission. Again and again... now... Quiet Storm stood in the Manhattan bookstore. She held that same book in her hands and felt the years fold in on themselves.

The distance between who she had been and who she had become seemed to vanish. Only the raw living center of her remained... the part Johnny's words always seemed to find. She lifted her gaze from his page for a moment.

She let the words echo through her frame... yes. Her skin tightened and rose. The store sounds faded into a soft blur.

Somewhere behind her... the bell on the door had chimed when he entered. Somewhere behind her... his presence had begun to move through the room. Her body knew before she did.

The air felt thicker and more alive... as if the world itself had taken a step closer. It did not ask... it stayed... yes. Quiet Storm had been moved by the man and the author long before she ever met him.

She had fallen for the way he named what she had buried. He had lit a single luminous candle in each of her sacred and private rooms. She had fallen for the feeling of being known by someone who did not know her name.

Yet somehow he knew her inner weather. Now... standing with *The Rare Flower* in her hands... she felt something else. Something much more important had arrived.

Her body remembered... yes... who he truly was to her. Not a celebrity and not a name on a cover. A presence.

A pure resonating frequency. A man whose words had already entered her body and rearranged her internal map. Yes... a man that only through his words had reset Quiet Storm's inner compass.

She did not know yet that he was standing only a few steps away. She only knew that the ground beneath her inner world tilted. Nothing inside her would ever again sit quite the same.

It recalibrated... yes... quietly... beneath her composure.

Something inside her shifted position... shifted majorly and could not return. What moved did not seek explanation.

It simply remained... present and very alive. It was adjusting the space around her without resolution. Yes... it called for her participation in her own life.

Outside the bookstore New York City continued its pace. It was unaware that something had been named in the universe without being spoken. Not yet.

What is named in the body and the soul does not hurry. It stays... yes... permanently... waiting for life to catch up. Recognition... once awakened... refuses to sleep again.

As the realization of his presence anchored her... Johnny unconsciously placed his **hand over his heart**. He felt the resonance of her soul's response. Then... he **rubbed his forearm** with a slow... grounded motion and chose to **detach**... letting the destiny of the moment hold its own hand.

CHAPTER THREE

The Moment the World Tilted

She closed the book halfway and held it against her chest for a breath. Around her... the low noise of the store continued... but she felt cocooned inside the ordinary sounds. Clarity lived in the secret pressed between her palms... hidden in plain sight from anyone watching.

Once she stood there... a well-mannered and well-dressed woman... something deeper had already begun to move. Now the atmosphere shifted... not dramatically... yet her entire body felt it. Guided by the pulse of the room... something unseen had stepped into her awareness.

Reality shifted as perhaps... yes... the most significant person in her life had entered in without asking permission. Underneath the weight of the moment... she felt the quiet summons that does not announce itself. Everything about it carried a weight that could not be refused once felt.

Now something deep inside her intuitively recognized that this shift within her was her subpoena. Coming forward... this was not a coincidence and not a choice she had made. Everything about it settled as the hairs on her arms lifted almost imperceptibly with subtle electricity.

The electricity moved and pulsated over and under her skin... through her inner thighs... flaring her senses. Her breath paused at the top of her lungs from a precognition that arrived directly from her unconscious. She felt this sensation before she even became conscious of its source.

Quiet Storm sensed... yes... felt him before she saw him... a significant presence. He was grounded... weathered... wise... moving into her awareness and brushing the edges of her sacred protective bubble. She had been willfully blind to the truth rising deep within her until this moment.

Without asking permission... it was not curiosity that stirred her... it was recognition arriving ahead of consent. Her body responded as if the decision had already been made somewhere beyond time. She no longer questioned... yes.

It pushed against her... rearranging how the room felt and then rearranging something deep inside her. She lifted her eyes... slowly... as if something within her already knew that once she looked... she could not go back. Their gazes met across the short distance between the shelves.

The hesitation carried meaning... yes... because crossing this invisible threshold would rearrange the internal order she had spent years constructing. She had spent decades fortifying and rigidly defending this space. She knew this without language as her mind registered what her body already knew.

The man standing near the display table was the man whose name she had just traced with her fingertips. She felt the choice arrive before she was asked to make it. She could look away and remain who she had been or stay present and allow the rearrange.

He was the man whose words had been the quiet witness of her inner fantasies and her most intimate projections. He was the man who understood her most untamed emotional weather from inside her body. Johnny Meadows was here... in the same real place... looking directly at her.

His presence did not intrude... it reorganized her demeanor as the space subtly recalibrated. Her first instinct was to shield herself behind the calm expression she had perfected in courtrooms. Her shoulders remained relaxed and her chin was quietly lifted.

Yet inside... something cracked... in a breaking that lets light enter through walls. She could not read his expression... seeing only a softness she did not expect. Beneath that sat a stillness that felt less like he was looking at her and more like he was entering her.

She had known now that she had bonded with the author of her deepest desires long before she ever saw him in the flesh. Time did not stop... yet it changed shape for her. Quiet Storm felt her heartbeat in the hollow of her throat and against her heart.

The pulse moved deep within her inner thighs as her fingers tightened around the book. She pressed the cover close against her chest... ignoring her training to move casually. Another part of her needed to step closer.

Her body already knew and she recognized the impulse as dangerous because it felt true. She simply held his gaze for one more breath that carried consequence. In that breath... something passed between them that had no language.

Recognition met recognition... yes... soul met soul. This was not attraction discovering itself... this was memory resurfacing. A real man who had stepped out of his own shadow stood before her.

They did not smile or speak as two inner worlds realized they were no longer alone. It felt as if this moment had been written long before this fated encounter. The world receded... yes.

This was the moment epic stories are built upon and passed down through the generations. The instant before the familiar collapses and something larger steps forward. She sensed that nothing profound ever begins without first unsettling the ground.

Johnny moved toward her with the unhurried cadence of

a man who did not need to prove himself. His steps were measured... grounded... and assured. He carried an internal quiet that reached her before his words could.

Again... and again... now... she felt his deep inner peace and certainty in her chest. It was warm and unsettling... thrusting through her middle body in ways she could never before imagined. Johnny stopped at a respectful distance to allow the energy to remain intact.

His restraint carried intention as he allowed her to arrive. The air felt denser around them... charged with something that caused her to tremble. Quiet Storm lifted her chin slightly in an instinctive gesture of desired surrender.

Her posture remained immaculate... yet her heartbeat betrayed her by pulsing visibly at the base of her throat. She saw his eyes notice it without judgment. He understood the part of her that struggled between staying composed and surrendering.

She had known then that he was not there to persuade or seduce her. He was there to reveal her to herself. That recognition carried far more power than pursuit ever could.

He nodded once... a subtle acknowledgment that landed deeper than any greeting in her life. She felt the nod in her chest... not her mind. Johnny's presence carried the weight of a man who had gone through fire and returned.

He possessed complete **CONGRUENCE** in his manner and a softened soul. She sensed this in the way he held himself... the calm steadiness of a man with nothing to chase. He just was present and comfortable in his own skin.

"You were drawn to it..." Johnny said quietly while his eyes returned to her face. His voice made her feel simultaneously exposed and held. "That is usually how it begins."

She did not trust her voice immediately as the words felt delicate and unfirm. She swallowed softly and then answered with a steadiness she did not entirely feel. "I have read your book before."

Johnny's tone was professional... yet beneath it he could

hear something she did not intend to reveal. He tilted his head slightly... listening for the truth beneath her words. He stepped half a breath closer... just enough for her senses to register his nearness.

She felt the warmth of him in the small gap like a hand pressing at the curve of her lower back. Her pulse quickened again... and this time she did not try to hide it. "You read it differently this time..." Johnny said.

She exhaled in a way that gave her away. Her eyes lowered for a moment and then lifted to find his calm confidence and warmth. He made her feel seen at a depth most women will never reach.

Quiet Storm tried to offer something safe... but the truth slipped through her restraint. "Yes..." she said softly. The truth landed low in her body before it reached her mind.

It settled where decisions form long before words appear. Johnny's eyes softened... though he did not smile... because smiling would have broken the spell. Silence settled between them with intention.

This was the kind of silence that marks a threshold moment before something irreversible is crossed. Instead... he let the truth settle between them like a quiet acknowledgment. He glanced down at the book in her hands and then gently back at her.

"Stories change when we do..." he said... his voice firm and low. "Sometimes they show us parts of ourselves we were not ready to see before." Her breath caught... enough for him to feel it.

She held the book tighter against her heart... as if anchoring herself from the pull. It was something deeper... archetypal... the kind a woman experiences when she meets a man who carries her emotional language. She felt the quiet fear that accompanies truth.

It was the fear of what would be required if she accepted what her body already knew. The part of her that had been dormant for years stirred awake. "You write as if you have lived a thousand lives..." she said quietly.

She wanted to know how he saw the things she thought no one else saw. He held her gaze with a calm that drew the air from her lungs. "Sometimes..." he said... "a man only needs to live one life deeply."

Her world did not shatter... it tilted. It tilted just enough to ensure it would never return to its previous alignment. Her knees nearly weakened.

She steadied herself with a slow inhale... clutching the book slightly tighter. He noticed the subtle softening of her shoulders and the delicate surrender she was trying to resist. His attention did not press against her... it received her.

That difference disarmed her more than anything he could have done. "Would you like it signed..." Johnny asked... "or is this one meant to be kept the way it was?" The question unraveled her in places she never allowed anyone to reach.

Her fingers brushed the cover and she felt heat move up through her inner thighs. It moved toward her breasts and her inner pelvis sensually awakened. He waited without impatience or pressure... and his restraint completely undid her.

Finally... she spoke... "Yes... I would like it signed if you will." Johnny nodded once... slow and deliberate... as if accepting something far greater than a request. "Then come..." he said gently. "We will sign it together."

Johnny's invitation carried weight because it asked for nothing and presumed nothing. It simply opened a door within her and trusted her to decide whether to cross. Quiet Storm's breath caught again.

Something in the resonance of his voice reached places deep inside her that had not been touched in years. She stepped forward without realizing she had moved. And that was the moment she surrendered to the beginning.

There would be no returning to who she had been before this step. The story had accepted her. At that moment... yes... unconsciously... Quiet Storm felt the truth settle low in her body.

She had fallen for this writer long before she ever looked into his eyes. Johnny guided her toward the small wooden table. He walked beside her with an ease that made the world around them feel distant.

The world slowed down as he listened to what her body was saying. Quiet Storm felt her breath adjust to the rhythm of his steps. It was as if her body was learning a new internal rhythm without her permission.

She tried to maintain her composed exterior... yet her awareness of him filled every inch of space. The air felt warmer now... shaped by something unspoken yet unmistakable. It felt true and honest.

He pulled the chair out gently for her... a gesture done without the hollow chivalry she was accustomed to. She sat slowly... grateful for the momentary pause to reflect upon this man. Johnny remained standing... his hand lightly brushing the table as he reached for a pen.

The movement was simple... yet she sensed intention in the slowness of it. She needed to really feel the moment rather than rush through it. Her heart lifted into her throat again... delicate and vulnerable.

Johnny opened the book to its inside cover and looked at the blank page. His handwriting was deliberate... anchored... and charactered. It was shaped by a man who had learned to do nothing carelessly.

She watched the slow glide of his pen and felt a tightness build in her chest. The sensation rose up through the center of her inner thighs. She had met authors before... yet she had never felt this sense of being drawn in.

She was entering the private world of a man whose words had already rearranged her inner map. The quiet between them felt too sacred to disturb. Quiet Storm felt it awakening within her... a feminine primordial knowing.

When he finished writing... Johnny closed the book and placed his hand on the cover. His fingertips rested near hers without touching. The small gap between their hands felt charged with subtle heat.

It was a connective unseen energy. He looked into her eyes and his expression held a quiet stillness. It made her feel both exposed and safe.

"This signature and inscription are for you..." he said gently. His voice carried warmth that settled into her being like a soft flame. "Not for the audience... not for the world... only for you... Quiet Storm."

She felt the words move through her... sinking into her with slow longing. Her fingers brushed the corner of the book and she felt her pulse in her breasts. It ran down her spine and then deep within her inner body.

Her voice wavered before she steadied it... "Thank you..." she said softly. The words felt insufficient for the weight of what she was feeling deep inside. She wished she could say more or simply retreat.

As the signature dried... Johnny unconsciously placed his **hand over his heart**. He felt the alignment of their shared purpose lock into place. Then... he **rubbed his forearm** with a slow... grounded motion and chose to **detach** from the peak intensity.

Johnny slid the book toward her with a quiet finality... then stepped back half a breath. It created a small shift in the space that allowed her to breathe. She looked down at the cover... then up at him with a depth she could not hide.

Recognition flickered through her like a distant memory. He received that depth without flinching. Something in him felt strangely familiar.

"Some encounters are fated... meant to happen..." Johnny said. His tone was prophetic... firm... and grounded. "Even when we do not expect them."

The words settled over her with the weight of truth. She felt something warm rise beneath her breasts... something she had kept dormant. Her breath deepened as she held the book close to her breasts once more.

The moment felt like the beginning of a thread pulling her toward the places she had avoided. She stood slowly... her body feeling lighter than when she had entered the bookstore. She lifted the book with both hands... unsure of whether to stay or walk away.

Johnny watched her with a calm that gave her the space to choose. His presence remained firm... offering no pressure and no chase. It was the kind of presence that made her feel seen without being captured.

She then felt a deep longing for her submission... to a man... to this man. She gave a small nod... the kind you offer when words cannot contain the truth. Johnny returned it with equal softness.

She turned toward the door as the atmosphere of the bookstore adjusted around her. Before she reached the exit... she paused... letting the moment breathe. Then she turned.

Johnny was still watching her with recognition that felt ancient and familiar. Quiet Storm felt her pulse stir once more. She stepped out into the Manhattan air with the book pressed to her breasts.

For the first time... she did not feel alone inside her own weather. She had fallen for the words long before she discovered the man. What she carried now was not infatuation... it was complete alignment.

The words had led her exactly where they were meant to land. The cosmic call had been made and the threshold had been revealed. Her life had already begun to change... yes... permanently.

The moment did not rush forward. What had occurred did not require pursuit or explanation. It had already crossed from encounter into meaning.

The body knew this before the mind attempted to organize it. Meaning... once embodied... does not ask whether it is welcome. It simply stays and grows.

Now... it anchored her... yes... quietly... beneath the surface of breath and posture. What shifted did not announce itself. It simply altered the internal balance she had relied on for years.

Something had been recognized and allowed to remain. It was just present... waiting... steady. And what settles like this does not retreat when the room changes.

CHAPTER FOUR

The One Her Soul Remembered

Johnny remained near the doorway of the bookstore as Quiet Storm stepped into the street... outside of time. His presence was firm behind her while he allowed the moment to move without interference. Clarity arrived because he did not follow and he did not call her back.

Once he stood still and let her go... yes... he was trusting that whatever had begun now lived inside both of them. Now what he did not follow... he had already entered. Guided by the presence they shared... the threshold had been crossed not by movement but by being.

Reality was such that her body carried the mark of him forward without asking her... yes... permission. Underneath the surface... it settled... yes... quietly... beneath posture and breath. Everything was moving beneath the habits she trusted to keep her protected and fragmented.

Now what entered her did not feel new but remembered... as if something long dormant had recognized its counterpart. Coming forward... what enters this way does not require pursuit... it roots.

Everything changed as he watched her disappear into the flow of the city and felt the impulse to move rise once.

He did not obey it. He let his breath settle into his chest and chose restraint as the only honest power he carried. Then he turned back toward the store as if nothing had happened... yes... while knowing everything had.

He walked to the table where he had signed her copy and placed the pen down with deliberate calm. He looked at the empty space where she had stood and allowed the silence to hold its weight. His jaw stayed relaxed and his shoulders stayed grounded.

He did not need to chase a woman to claim meaning... yes... and he did not need to speak more to make the moment real. Quiet Storm stepped onto the busy Manhattan sidewalk with the book pressed firmly against her breasts. It was as if the warmth of his presence had settled into the cover itself.

The morning air brushed her skin with a coolness that should have grounded her... yet her inner edges felt loosened. Her body already knew... yes. She moved through the noise of the city with practiced composure... yes.

None of it reached her fully because the imprint of the bookstore still traveled through her body. This was no longer curiosity... or admiration... or fantasy. Something had claimed her attention from beneath thought... and it did not recede when she told herself to keep walking.

Her posture remained precise and upright... the posture of a woman who knew how to hold herself. Each breath revealed a tenderness she could not quite conceal... a quiet tremor at the hollow of her throat. It slid down her spine and moved behind her breasts.

The sensation settled lower... yes... gathering as a soft ache near her pelvis and inner thighs. The book felt heavier in her hands as she walked... almost alive with its quiet weight. It carried more than ink and paper.

It carried his signature and the memory of his eyes when he

wrote it for her. She traced the edge of the pages with her thumb in a slow rhythm... yes. She was trying to anchor herself in texture while warmth hummed beneath her skin.

Her thoughts attempted to restore order the way she had trained them to for years. She reminded herself that she had met writers before and that admiration for a mind did not equal destiny. She told herself she had known the difference between story and reality... yes.

Yet those thoughts thinned each time the calm focus of his gaze returned to her. She kept walking and refused to look back... even though her body pulled and needed to. The refusal made her shoulders tighten as if she had drawn a line through herself.

She told herself that looking back would invite something she could not control. The book pressed against her breasts like a hand she did not grant permission to... yes. Her breath deepened anyway as she walked.

She paused at the crosswalk as traffic surged past in sound and motion. The memory of him stepping closer returned with unsettling truth... the way his presence entered her space without hurry. Her hand lifted to rest lightly over her breasts as warmth gathered again... yes.

Then the sensation slid downward through her loins toward her inner thighs. The light changed and she stepped forward more from habit than intention. Her body knew the route home... yet her awareness stayed in the quiet stretch of time.

She remembered handing him the book he had written... The Rare Flower. She could still feel the fragile thread between their hands as he took the book... yes. It was a line that felt more like recognition than coincidence.

It felt like pure synchronicity. The quiet poetry of life was arranging itself around an unseen truth. Meaning arrives without explanation and recognition replaces reason.

Quiet Storm remembered how his eyes softened without losing their steadiness and warmth. There had been no performance within him... only a quiet knowing. It reached toward the part of her she had learned to keep hidden.

The memory of his hand holding the pen sent another shiver through her... moving down her spine. It settled again as a tender pull near her inner thighs... yes. It was as if her body retained the echo of his touch.

A simple truth rose inside her... slow and unmistakable. She had not been stirred by a fantasy projected onto a stranger. She had been moved by him... yes... by the man behind the words.

Her soul had known his presence before her mind caught up. That truth did not flatter her... it threatened her. She drew a measured breath as if gathering scattered pieces of herself.

Beneath her composed stride... a new stillness formed... not the stillness of retreat but the stillness of something real. Her body had answered him first... yes. She could no longer pretend that answer did not matter.

The answer had already been given before she knew there was a question. Whatever followed would not be decided by caution... but by truth. Still... she tried to stay in control.

She lowered her gaze to the book and felt its weight shift in her hands. It carried a quiet vow she had not agreed to yet. His signature inside no longer felt routine or polite.

It felt intentional... yes... like a private exchange her body treated as real. Her thumb brushed the cover and warmth rose behind her breasts before moving lower. A gentle ache formed deep in her inner thighs.

Her steps slowed without conscious choice. She heard herself acknowledge that he was different. Something about him felt already woven into her story... yes... deep into her soul.

The admission never reached her lips... yes... yet it traveled through her body with unmistakable authority. It was a deep truth. She did not argue with it... she only tightened around it.

She reached her building with the same outward composure her neighbors always saw. She greeted the doorman with a soft nod and familiar kindness. Even he sensed something had shifted... yes.

There was a softer light in her eyes as if a hidden place had begun to thaw. She hated that anyone could see it. The elevator doors closed and the small space intensified everything.

She pressed the button for her floor and leaned lightly against the wall. The book was still cradled against her breasts. Warmth gathered beneath her blouse and slid downward... yes.

It settled into a subtle ache near her pelvis and inner thighs that refused to be ignored. She inhaled and felt her mouth go dry. She tightened her fingers around the spine of the book.

She allowed her breath to deepen instead of retreating. For once she did not numb what her body was communicating... she surrendered fully. She let the heat rise and fall with each inhale... yes.

The ache settled as information rather than threat. The elevator rose and she felt as if she was rising with it toward a life that might not stay intact. The doors opened and she walked down the hallway.

She unlocked her apartment and stepped into the careful order she had built. The silence wrapped around her like a familiar coat... yes. Today it felt much thinner... as if his presence had followed her inside.

She closed the door and felt the click land behind her breasts. She set her purse down and placed her keys in the small dish. The act steadied her briefly before her attention returned to the book.

She carried it to the kitchen island and set it down gently... yes. It was the way one sets something that holds more than its form. Morning light spilled across the cover and made the title glow.

She traced the edge of the book with slow fingertips and felt warmth stir. It traveled from her breasts down her spine and deepened. There was a quiet pull toward her lower body and inner thighs.

The contrast between the cool countertop and the heat within her made her swallow deeply... yes. None of this felt abstract. It felt like a door inside her had cracked wide open.

She filled a glass with water and drank slowly... hoping for grounding. The coolness eased her throat and changed nothing else. Heat continued to move through her with quiet authority... yes.

It was unbothered by reason. She set the glass down and felt her fingers tremble for a moment. She walked to the window and rested one hand against the glass.

Manhattan moved below without noticing her. She felt the contrast between motion and stillness. She had built her life on restraint... yet what stirred now did not feel reckless... yes.

It felt right. It felt like the part of her that always knew she was meant to experience more. She tried once more to talk herself away from it.

She told herself she did not know him and that moments could deceive. She told herself that longing was not evidence and that bodies could be wrong. Her body answered with a deeper... yes... harder warmth.

It was a fuller ache low in her center... yes... an answer that refused debate. She reached for her phone and held it for a long breath. Her thumb hovered over the screen.

She imagined a polite line... a safe line that would keep her above her own desire. Then she felt the heat deepen and she set the phone back down... yes. She was choosing silence because silence felt safer than truth.

That choice did not calm her... it tightened her. She felt it at her neck first... then at her shoulders. Finally... it moved lower where her body stayed honest.

Control had always been her virtue... yet control now tasted like fear. She closed her eyes and admitted that fear had been shaping her life. He had touched it without touching her.

She turned back to the island as if drawn by gravity. She opened the cover and saw his handwriting... firm and warm and calm. Her breath paused just above her breasts... yes.

Something in the inscription landed exactly where she guarded most. It was simple... and that simplicity felt like a hand that did not squeeze. It was inviting her to walk through a door she had locked long ago.

That door led back to herself. Quiet Storm's fingertips moved along each line as though tracing a holy scripture. It felt received before language and sealed into the flesh.

The ink did not shimmer... yet it felt alive because it carried his steadiness. It carried a masculine warmth... yes... his calm. She closed the book and held it against her breasts.

She felt her heartbeat meet the cover. The rhythm traveled downward and settled again near her pelvis... yes. It was as if her body needed to keep him in there.

Quiet Storm stood in the kitchen and listened to the quiet of her apartment. It was the quiet she had once called peace. It did not feel like serenity today... it felt like a room after a truth has been spoken.

She realized she had been alone in the corner for a long time. She had been safe... yes. She had been starving emotionally her entire adult life because fear had quietly replaced living.

She had mistaken survival for peace. It lingered... yes... like heat that refuses to cool. It was like a question the body answers before the mind consents.

Safety had been her discipline and hunger had been her silence. Now neither could pretend they did not know each other. What wakes this way does not quiet with rest... it waits.

She moved to the bedroom and placed the book on the nightstand. The room felt altered by her presence. It was as though it had been waiting for this version of her all her life.

She stood still and listened to her breath. Each inhale felt fuller than usual... as if the air itself had held her deepest secrets. She slipped out of her blouse.

She put on a soft cotton shirt that brushed her skin. Fabric grazed her breasts and traced downward... sending a trail of awareness. Her warmth deepened... yes... familiar and new all at once.

The cotton shifted against her nipples and her breath caught. It was as though her body had been waiting for that one unguarded friction... yes. The moment sensation stopped asking permission had arrived.

She sat on the edge of the bed and let her feet rest on the floor. The wood was cool beneath her soles and did not change the heat moving deep inside. She kept her hands in her lap and refused to touch herself.

She refused to ease the ache. The refusal made the sensation scream louder... yes. She understood that denial had always been a form of her control.

She leaned back against the headboard and closed her eyes. For years she had contained her depth beneath discipline and elegance. He had not asked for any of it... yes.

Still... something cracked wide open deep inside her. That opening did not feel like surrender to him... it felt like surrender to her own truth. When she opened her eyes again... seriousness had replaced confusion.

She knew something meaningful had been set in motion without promise. The ache low in her body no longer felt dangerous... yes... it felt true. Truth was the one thing she could never fully control.

She drew the book into her lap and let her hands curve around it. The scent of paper and ink carried him back into her awareness. It came with a force that did not shout.

Her breath slowed and deepened... yes. She welcomed the memory while her throat tightened as if she might cry. She did not cry... she only felt emotions she had been running from.

She pictured him as he stood... grounded and unhurried. Strength and softness coexisted in him without effort. That balance unsettled her more than charm ever could.

She remembered the calm line of his shoulders and the way his eyes did not flinch. Her heart answered with a firm beat that moved from her breasts to her inner loins... yes. It was reverent... sure... and peaceful.

As the stillness anchored her... she unconsciously placed her **hand over her heart**. She felt the alignment of her soul's truth. Then... she **rubbed her forearm** with a slow... grounded motion and chose to **detach** from the weight of her old defenses... letting the threshold remain open.

CHAPTER FIVE

The Thread That Already Lived Inside Her

Johnny stepped out of the café with the quiet confidence of a man who shaped the rhythm of the morning simply by walking through it. Clarity arrived as the air held a coolness that brushed across his face with firm truth. Once he began to walk... his steps moved in an unhurried cadence that revealed an inner world untouched by noise.

Now he sensed a shift inside himself... yes... the kind of shift that settles when something true begins to form beneath thought. Guided by the memory of Quiet Storm... he paused at the street corner as taxis streaked past. Reality was such that he lifted his gaze toward the soft sky and let the light settle across his well-defined features.

Underneath his mind... his awareness moved without force toward the quiet pride in her posture and the vulnerability behind her eyes. Every part of him felt the recognition rise again in his chest... warm and firm... yes. Now he felt the kind of truth that does not fade with time... only becoming stronger as he walked toward Central Park.

Coming toward the stillness... he understood silence more

deeply than words as the path opened before him in green and gold tones. Everything about the slower rhythm gathered around him... yes... the kind of rhythm only a man rooted in himself could absorb. He found a bench near the pond and seated himself with relaxed shoulders.

His hands rested on his lap and his breath moved in long grounded cycles. He felt the memory of her presence ripple through him... soft yet certain... yes... it comforted him in that moment. He did not chase the meaning but allowed it to rise in its own time.

Truth never needed pressure to reveal itself as he watched the water with contemplative calm. His near-death experience in 2019 had taught him that real peace lived in honest breath. Johnny carried that truth now with every quiet inhale.

His awareness drifted toward her again with gentle inevitability. He sensed that something inside her had opened in their brief exchange... yes. It was a door she kept guarded until a man with depth approached it without fear.

He held this recognition with deep respect. Johnny leaned back and let his head rest against the bench. The thought of her did not stir longing... it stirred knowing... yes.

Certain women enter a man's awareness with a presence that does not leave when the moment ends. He understood that he had encountered such a woman. The truth settled into his breath... then deeper... where he allowed it to rest.

The wind shifted and he opened his eyes. He felt a small certainty form inside his chest that he did not question. Slowly... inevitably... he sensed it... yes.

He trusted the knowing that he would see her again. The thread that connected them tightened in silence... yes... a silence older than thought. It was older than the universe itself and outside of time... yes.

He rose from the bench and continued along the winding path.

This was no longer something he could notice and set aside. It had shifted into direction.

This deep knowing did not ask for his preference or permission. It settled deep within him and quietly began to influence where his attention moved. From this point forward awareness would no longer be passive.

It would carry weight... and weight always brings consequence. Johnny paused where the light reached the ground and stopped. Stillness lived there without comfort or invitation.

The memory of the bookstore returned and settled through him without sentiment... only truth. Her eyes spoke the language of depth buried beneath composure and well-practiced surfaces... yes. Her life was engineered to appear complete while remaining hollow.

He recognized that language because he had lived inside it himself. He had endured it long before the near-death experience shattered his illusions. It ended the outer world he had mistaken for substance.

Johnny did not resent that ending... he had received it... yes. He accepted it as inevitable rather than personal. Every stripping away had been required.

Every loss had carried a great life learning and nothing had been wasted. This too belonged to the path... the cost of refusing to live half awake. It was the discipline exacted by a full and complete life.

Johnny moved on with an ease others felt without understanding. Men noticed his calm and women felt the quiet pull he carried... yes. It was a pull born from grounded presence rather than a fake performance.

He reached the edge of the park and stepped back into the city. When he arrived at his publisher's building he entered the elevator with collected steadiness. His composure remained intact.

The meeting went smoothly. When he spoke... he carried the **CONGRUENCE** and conviction of a man who understood truths. He knew that stories are born from both internal and eternal sources.

Her presence rose in his awareness again... yes... not as a distraction. It was an alignment recognized at the level of the soul. He sensed she would play a role in the next chapter of his creative life.

Perhaps... yes... in his personal life as well. He left the building and stepped into the moving stream of people outside. He moved with unbroken calm and clear inner direction.

His outer movement matched his inner state. He was a man who had become one... congruent. He felt a pull beneath his breath.

It was subtle yet unmistakable. He had encountered a woman who would not fade from his awareness... yes. This was a recognition that rose from a place inside him that only spoke when something ancient had been touched.

The knowing settled in his chest like a vow older than time itself. Johnny walked north and allowed the feeling to take its place inside him. A memory surfaced from long ago.

The tulips of the Dutch Golden Age returned to his thoughts. These were the broken tulips treasured for the fractures that created colors no other flower dared to hold. The Queen of Night had been the rarest of them all... a near black bloom.

It drew the world toward its depth. It held beauty shaped by accident and time. It held mystery shaped by rarity and endurance.

He felt the resonance now... yes. Quiet Storm carried that same impossible essence. She was a singular bloom shaped by forces older than reason and... yes... older than time.

Her presence had moved through him the moment she looked at him. Her eyes revealed more than she spoke. He carried that recognition in his breath now.

He turned onto a side street lined with art galleries. A painting of a near black tulip waited in the window. It stood with the quiet authority of something that had already chosen who would receive it.

Johnny stepped inside and approached the canvas with measured steps. The depth of the petals echoed the depth he had seen in Quiet Storm's gaze. He absorbed the stillness and allowed the recognition... yes... to take root deep within him... now.

Johnny purchased the painting and stepped out into the street. He carried the calm certainty of a man who understood synchronicity. Symbols appeared only when the internal world was ready to receive them.

He walked toward the park again... holding the quiet shift inside him with respect. Quiet Storm believed in synchronicity as well. She felt it beneath her breath and in her inner loins.

It lived in the quiet spaces where intuition spoke before thought. She felt it in the symbols that arrived only when her soul softened enough to see them. The encounter with him lived in her body now.

Yes... she felt it deep in her pelvis and along the warm pull gathering in her inner thighs. Her body decided. The universe had placed him in her path when she was ready to receive what she had long avoided.

The thread neither had named was already alive. What stirred in him echoed in her. What awakened in her mirrored him.

The universe had chosen its moment and spoke in feeling rather than logic... yes. It spoke through recognition instead of reason. Johnny paused at the entrance to the park and felt the truth deepen within him.

The Queen of the Night... yes... the black tulip painting had confirmed what he already sensed... yes... knew. Something rare had entered his path and did not intend to leave. He continued through the park toward a small bridge.

He rested his hands on the railing and allowed the stillness to reveal truth to him. His near-death experience rose in his awareness and grounded him. Nothing real was fragile and nothing true required force.

The painting lived in his mind with quiet weight... yes. It was the same weight he felt when he first saw Quiet Storm in the bookstore. He stepped off the bridge and walked toward the park exit.

Her presence rested quietly in the space behind each step. It was not a distraction but an alignment... yes. This was the alignment he trusted over everything else.

He carried that awareness with him as he walked toward his hotel. When he entered his room he placed the painting near the window. He stood in silence and let his breath move through him.

The day had carried a shift he could not deny. Something in him had moved toward a truth he trusted. He rested in the awareness that Quiet Storm lived somewhere in that truth now... yes.

She was alive in the place inside him that only destiny would be allowed to reach. Johnny sat in the chair by the window and closed his eyes. The memory of her rose in the softest part of his awareness.

Yes... it remained. It moved through his chest and settled there as if it had always belonged. He did not resist the knowing... he welcomed it.

The thread between them did not need shape or logic. It needed only breath... yes. It required the quiet acceptance of two souls recognizing something older than themselves... yes... deep within each other.

He let the evening gather around him with unbroken calm. He felt her presence inside him in a way that did not disrupt his peace. She lived there now as a gentle pulse... yes... a pulse that aligned with his breath.

The thread remained unbroken. It waited for its moment to rise again. It waited for her and it waited for him.

It waited for what already lived inside them both. The thread did not tighten or pull... yes... it simply remained. It lived beneath decision and beyond effort.

It was adjusting the way stillness felt and the way absence no longer meant separation. What recognizes itself once does not need pursuit. It waits... already alive and already moving.

As the realization anchored his presence... Johnny unconsciously placed his **hand over his heart**. He felt the pulse of the alignment lock into place. Then... he **rubbed his forearm** with a slow... grounded motion and chose to **detach** from the day... letting the thread wait for its season.

CHAPTER SIX

The Truth Stirring Her Awake

Quiet Storm woke before dawn with a sharp inhale... her body rising from sleep as though a hand had lifted her from the inside. She lay still beneath the sheets... now... then... now... then... sensing a warmth pressing low behind her breasts. Clarity gathered deeper through her inner thighs as it pulsed softly... yes... a slow awakening she could not guide or quiet.

Once she touched her breast gently... she felt a tremor beneath her palm... a quiet tightening that told her something had followed her into sleep. Now it stayed with her from the night while the room felt unchanged yet altered. Guided by a subtle charge across her skin... she breathed again... slower... trying to firm herself... yes.

Reality settled... but the tension remained as she rose with careful steps. Underneath the early softness of morning... she let the cool floor ground her while the silence wrapped around her. Every thought drifted into the pull rising in her breasts... as her nipples began to harden and her mind could not form its usual order.

Now the memory of the man from the bookstore... the writer

of her inner worlds... pressed into her deep. Coming forward... he had pressed sensually into her awareness before she could resist it. Everything stretched before her as she poured her coffee and moved to the window... familiar and firm... yet none of it settled her.

Her breath tightened again beneath her breasts... yes... as if a new part of her life had opened without her consent. She told herself it was nothing. Yet the truth gathered in her body... not her mind.

Something within her had been stirred awake... yes... in the very places she hid from the world. The harder she tried to deny it... the stronger the sensation grew. It rose through her inner thighs with a quiet insistence she could not reason away.

She whispered to herself that this could not be real... yet the truth trembled inside her with each breath. This was not fantasy... it was recognition... yes... the kind that lives beneath thought. She lifted the cup to her lips... but the warmth did nothing to comfort her.

She felt the memory of him return as an imprint rather than a thought... an echo that brushed the soft underside of her breasts. The sensation moved lower through her center. Her body spoke before her mind could catch up... yes... revealing a surrender she did not fully understand yet.

Quiet Storm closed her eyes. She had always trusted her intuition... even the parts she kept buried beneath discipline. And that intuition now told her with undeniable softness that the encounter had not been small.

It had reached something deep within her that had been asleep for more years than she could remember. She dressed with slow intention... feeling the air brush against her skin as though it carried his presence. Her reflection in the mirror looked unchanged... yet something behind her eyes held a depth she had not seen before.

She stepped out into the hallway and felt the shift move with her... yes... quiet but alive. By the time she reached her office building... her thoughts felt split between two realities. There was the world outside and the world he had awakened within her.

She entered the elevator... her colleagues fading into the background as her inner world pulsed louder than their voices. Quiet Storm closed her office door quietly behind her. The silence rose around her... yes... and with it the memory of him returned.

She felt her breath catch just above her breasts... before time began... not from fear... but from recognition. She sat at her desk... and the truth rose through her like a slow tide. Warmth moved along her spine... brushing lightly behind her breasts.

The heat deepened through her inner thighs with a gentle pressure that felt like a hand guiding her inward. She exhaled softly... yes... feeling a new part of herself open. Her emails blurred across the screen.

Words lost their meaning as her attention drifted back to the quiet moment in the bookstore. He had looked at her without reaching and something in that gaze had entered her. It was not through touch... but through presence... yes... a presence her body still held.

Quiet Storm inhaled and tried to focus. Yet each attempt only brought him back to her with greater truth. The memory of the steadiness and warmth in his eyes softened her from within.

His gaze brushed against her in ways she had never allowed. It unsettled her... and awakened her... yes... at the same time. The meeting that followed felt distant.

Her attention fractured as her body kept returning to the sensation rising from between her hips... yes... directly in the middle of her pelvis. Each pause allowed her awareness to fall deeper into the pull she had been resisting. Her body already knew... yes... the quiet pull that felt older than desire.

When the meeting ended... she returned to her office and closed the door quickly. She placed both hands on the desk to firm herself... yet the stillness only magnified what rose through her. She felt drawn to him with a depth she could not hide from herself... yes... even if she tried.

Quiet Storm moved to the window. The Manhattan skyline stretched before her yet felt unfamiliar... as though her world had been lifted and set down somewhere new. She let her breath settle... softening into the awareness she feared naming.

Something great in her had awakened. Something real and something hers had emerged. As the afternoon thinned into evening... she closed her laptop and let the quiet gather around her.

Her steps carried her toward the bookshelf on instinct rather than thought. Her fingertips brushed the spine of one of Johnny Meadows' earlier books. A soft ache rose through her chest... yes... deeper than she expected.

She remembered how his writing had once unsettled her in ways she had never admitted out loud. How it had reached into the hidden places she protected from everyone was now clear. The resonance returned now... brushing the hollow of her throat and the soft underside of her breasts... yes.

The feeling moved lower through her center. She closed her eyes... yes... letting the memory settle deep within her... now. She had not merely liked his work... she had recognized herself through it.

She had recognized him. And the truth that rose now felt like a return rather than a beginning. Quiet Storm walked into the hallway with a steadiness and false confidence she did not feel.

The elevator descended as her body pulsed with a quiet rhythm she could not ignore. Each breath drew the sensation higher... yes... revealing a shift already in motion. She stepped into the evening air and felt it touch her face with a softness that startled her.

At that moment... she felt him again... not in thought... but in presence. A subtle warmth gathered behind her breasts... yes... and moved lower through her inner world. Her surrender to that moment was instinctual... yes... primal.

It did not come from her mind. It came from the place inside her where truth lives. She crossed the street slowly... moving as though the world had shifted pace.

Her body reacted to something she could not see... yet felt with truth. She knew she had opened. She knew something inside her had stirred awake.

When she reached her apartment... she paused at the door. She sensed that stepping inside would not return her to the woman she had been. She opened the door slowly... exhaling as the silence rose around her and within her.

Quiet Storm leaned her hand against the wall to firm the shift moving through her. She sensed an awakening deep beneath her breath and... yes... deep beneath her breasts. This was an emergence she could no longer suppress.

She felt herself soften... yes... into the truth she had spent years avoiding and running from. She walked to the window and gazed at the city lights. They blurred softly as her inner world expanded.

She felt the same trembling she had felt in the bookstore... the same deep recognition brushing along her skin. It was not imagined. It lived deep inside her... yes... fully awakened now.

The thread between them pulsed faintly within her... as though something unseen had tied itself to her breath. It was not desire alone. It was pure recognition... yes... soul deep.

This named feeling was undeniable. Quiet Storm made a quiet decision... yes... a silent agreement with herself. She would follow the signs and the symbols and the synchronicities that had entered her life.

She would not retreat from them again. She sat on the edge of her bed and let her breath deepen. Warmth moved through her inner thighs... curling upward in slow waves she could not guide or... yes... suppress.

She felt the shift settle inside her like an ancient truth returning... yes... a truth she had been waiting to remember. Quiet Storm closed her eyes. The day replayed itself in soft fragments... each one carrying his presence beneath it.

She felt traces of him in the air... brushing the soft places she tried to hide herself from. Since their fated meeting... something had changed within her shadow... yes. Its grip had loosened its hold on her.

The truth moved through her gently and undeniably. Something had opened and something had begun. She knew with the quiet honesty she reserved only for herself... it could not be undone.

Yes... some deeper rhythm within her had already decided they would meet again. What stirred did not settle into understanding or resolve... yes. It simply remained present beneath her breath and behind her choices.

Recognition did not fade with rest or repetition. It lingered quietly... altering what stillness felt like and what absence could no longer erase. Quiet Storm stood at the window and felt the truth move through her without resistance.

As the realization of her awakening centered her... Quiet Storm placed her **hand over her heart**. She felt the pulse of the truth she could no longer deny. Then... she **rubbed her forearm** with a slow... grounded motion and chose to **detach** from her old fears... letting the transformation complete itself.

It did not ask her to understand it or explain it or name it. It simply settled beneath her breath and changed the way stillness felt.

CHAPTER SEVEN

The Man Behind
The Words

Johnny walked through Manhattan at night with the quiet certainty of a man who had rebuilt himself from the bottom up. Clarity lived in the city that glowed like distant constellations while the traffic buzzed like a restless tide. Once he began to move... his footsteps were firm on the pavement and unhurried.

Now each step carried the weight of years that most individuals would never see written on his face. Guided by purpose... he was not a man looking for distractions or superficial comforts. Reality was such that he moved like a man who had already faced the deepest silence and made peace with it.

Underneath the solitude... he felt a presence that strengthened rather than hollowed him. Every part of him remembered the time when the adults in his life failed to protect him. Now he recalled being the boy who could not follow the lines on the page in primary school.

Coming upon the classrooms of his past... he felt the shame creep up the back of his neck as meaning slid away like sand. Everything about the world had already decided who he was and what he was capable of. He learned very young that silence was safer than asking for help.

He believed he was broken because no one told him he was not. Again... and again... now... that belief planted itself deep inside him. It was shaping the landscape of his early soul.

The label was not spoken out loud... yet he felt it in every sigh and impatient correction. Words like Stupid... Slow... and Dyslexic sat in the air around him like invisible dust. He began to retreat... not in anger... but in quiet surrender.

If no one could see what lived inside him... he would protect it by hiding it. The loneliness of those years became the first room in his inner house. Even now... walking through Manhattan... he could still feel its high walls.

His childhood ended the day his parents sent him away to boarding school... yes... at eleven years old. Robert Land Academy... yes... Canada's only military school. The buildings rose out of the land like a War of 1812 fort.

The first time he saw it... he felt the air change. The military school's fort walls were the threshold that this eleven-year-old boy crossed over into a living hell. Inside this living hell... softness was a major liability.

Mornings came in the dark with shouted orders and boots hitting the ground in hard unison. The freezing wind cut across the parade square during winter without mercy. Discipline was not a suggestion... it was his daily reality.

Without asking permission... it was the air he breathed. He watched boys cry into their pillows at night and then wake up and put on their uniforms. Punishments were sharp and simple and unquestioned.

There were no hiding places and no one cared about the fragile parts of a boy's heart. Yet something in Johnny refused to die... a quiet ember beneath the cold. He bent in those years... badly... but he refused to break.

The long marches through mud and the drills until his muscles ripped carved him down to his essence. He learned that he could be pushed beyond what he thought he could bear and still keep standing. He learned that he could be punished and humiliated yet remain whole.

There was still a small unbroken core inside him that did not belong to anyone else. Yes... there was a part of him that even the harshest punishment could not touch. In this moment... then... here... it became the anchor of his masculine presence.

He noticed which boys turned hard and which boys quietly grew strong. Some boys took on the cruelty around them and became mirrors of it. Others folded in on themselves and never came back.

Johnny watched and listened and paid attention carefully to how pain changed people. He was still the boy who struggled with reading... yet he learned to read storms in other people's eyes. He began to understand that every human being is fighting a battle no one can see.

That understanding stayed with him longer than any uniform ever could. It was shaping the gentleness beneath his weathered exterior. By the time he left... the world thought it had reshaped him.

They saw the discipline and the straight shoulders and the controlled posture. They did not see the quiet oath he made to himself. He would never use power to crush another person's spirit.

He had seen too much of that. He would take the resilience and the endurance and use it to protect rather than to dominate. If life was going to be hard... then he would refuse to become hard in the same way.

Between the ages of eleven and fifteen Johnny made a quiet promise to take his own path. He would not move with the crowd simply because it was easy or familiar. He would question what others accepted without thought... yes.

He chose to walk quietly with a big stick. He did not use it for power or display it for fear. He carried it as a charge placed upon him... yes.

He would lift it only to protect himself or for others who could not protect themselves. That choice shaped his spine and his conscience. He learned that strength without restraint was chaos... yes... and restraint without strength was abandonment of one's soul.

His direction did not bend and his presence did not ask permission. He carried the calm authority of a man who understood protection and personal agency as a sacred duty. He honored it without spectacle.

His masculinity would not wound... it would firm. The years that followed looked successful from the outside as he learned how to pass exams. He learned how to speak in rooms where people wore suits and held fake smiles.

He built a career in a world of numbers and financial solutions. This world measured worth in titles and balance sheets. He became the man people trusted with their wealth and their fears.

His calendar filled and his reputation grew. He travelled and lectured and advised until his name began to carry its own weight. Yet somewhere deep inside him... the boy who once sat alone with backwards letters still whispered.

Something was always off-key. Building a life on achievement felt like building a house on sand. At night... when the noise finally quieted... he still felt like the boy who needed an Audience of One.

Not a crowd and not fans and certainly not sycophants. He needed one soul who could see him without the mask. He did not know her name... only the shape of the ache she left behind.

This was a quiet longing that lived inside him like an unfinished book. His life broke open on a morning that began like any other. He ignored the strange weakness in his limbs until his body simply refused to move.

The hospital came next with white light and urgent voices. There was the metallic smell of machines and the sharp taste of fear on the tongues of professionals. Numbers meant nothing except that he was in serious trouble.

His body had pulled the emergency brake his mind would not. Then the floor of his world gave way. His body slipped into a coma and the life he had been holding dissolved.

She let it happen…this was the true crossing. Not a metaphor and not a breakdown. It was a full descent beyond the point where identity could be negotiated.

The boy who had learned to endure was no longer enough here. Only total and complete surrender could pass him through. In that strange nowhere land… he watched the walls of his identity collapse.

His name and his accomplishments no longer mattered. The stories he had told himself melted like butter in sunlight. What remained was pure existence… stripped and silent.

What was left was not emptiness but a quiet and vast awareness. It did not belong to his career or his status or his past identity. He felt everything and nothing at once.

The boundary between him and the rest of existence grew thin and then vanished. The distance between the "I" and "the world" collapsed. He saw that most of what people agree is real is only a shared illusion.

The realization entered his body like gravity reversing… yes. It was collapsing the false center he had lived from and revealing a quieter axis beneath it. This could not be taught… only experienced firsthand.

The rules and the roles and the endless chase were all scaffolding. It was erected over something far more simple and far more true. He knew then that life was not asking him to achieve… but to align… yes.

He felt the weight of that knowing settle deep in his body… yes. It was not relief but responsibility. From that moment forward he would no longer measure himself by what he produced.

He would live from the inside outward... even if it cost him everything. It was asking him to awaken. When he woke... he was not afraid of death.

He opened his eyes and saw hospital walls... yet he also saw through them. He knew he could not go back to sleepwalking through his own life. The man who had gone into that coma had died.

What rose in his place stood still inside the space death had cleared. He understood that nothing from his former life could follow him intact. Whatever remained would have to be chosen consciously... breath by breath.

The man who woke up was someone else. He carried the same face and the same name... yet the axis inside him had shifted. What mattered now lived in a deeper territory of the soul.

He tried at first to fit this new self back into the old life. He attempted to carry on and be the husband and the professional. Yet deep down he knew something irrevocable had happened.

He looked at his days and saw how much energy had been spent chasing acceptance. He realized that so many of his choices were built on fear... not love. He knew in his bones that he could not betray what God had allowed him to see.

His marriage had already been fraying along invisible seams. Much of it had been built on good intentions and unspoken disappointments. When the chance came to move to San Diego... he agreed.

He treated it as a final act of faith to save what had been precious. He left Toronto where he had lived like a prince and people knew his work. He stepped into a life where he meant nothing to anyone.

In San Diego... he was just a man walking near the ocean trying to understand who he had become. The unfamiliarity felt strangely honest. The marriage did not survive the move.

Geography cannot mend a fracture that runs through the soul. He watched the union he had given decades to unravel thread by thread. It did not explode... it dissolved.

The ending hurt in ways that reached back into his childhood.

There were nights when grief sat on his chest like weight. Yet underneath the pain... another truth slowly surfaced.

He had been living as if his worth depended on being chosen. Now he understood that belonging had to be chosen from within. When the legal papers were done... he did not rush to replace what he had lost.

He did not throw himself into a new relationship or a bigger stage. He began to move through the world alone. He travelled and walked foreign streets at dusk and dawn.

He swam in oceans when most people were still sleeping. He ate simple meals and listened to the sound of his own breathing. He noticed how the panic of being alone gave way to stillness.

He discovered that solitude did not mean abandonment... it meant attention. His body already knew to pay attention to the moment and to his calling. He was sitting with his thoughts without running from them.

He realized that he had spent decades trying to be chosen. If he could not be his own best friend... he would never be any good for anyone else. Solitude became the forge that made him whole.

During those years... he started to write. He wrote the way a man opens a window in a room that has grown too tight. He poured out stories and quiet truths he had been carrying since the boy in the classroom.

Pages filled and then chapters. He was not trying to be an author... he was trying to breathe. His words became the bridge between his wounds and his wisdom.

The books took shape almost without his permission. One became two and two became six. Somewhere along the way... they left his hands and travelled far beyond him.

People read the words and reached out from different countries. They said that something in his writing had named what they had endured in silence. His words had reached places no one had reached.

The books moved without promotion or spectacle. They

appeared in boardrooms and courtrooms and on bedside tables. They were recommended privately and passed quietly.

His books became international bestsellers because recognition cannot be marketed. Tens of millions carried the books because something inside them resonated... yes. He had articulated a condition and named basic human truths.

He gave language to what many already lived but had never been allowed to name. His words did not comfort illusion... they dismantled it. And once illusion fell... alignment was no longer optional.

His name started to carry a new kind of weight anchored in meaning. This time... he did not take the bait. The praise did not intoxicate him because he had walked too close to death.

He accepted success with gratitude and distance. He valued the way his words found people... yet he refused to climb back onto the altar of external worship. He knew what it cost to build a life on being adored by strangers.

He was no longer willing to pay that price. Freedom required inner silence. He watched other men chase what he had once needed and saw the emptiness behind their eyes.

The mansions and the status dinners looked to him like glass... shiny and impressive and very fragile. He repeated a simple truth on nights when memory tried to draw him back. What you really want will almost never come to you when you are desperate for it.

When it finally does arrive... you may discover you no longer need it. Hunger distorts desire and fulfillment is rarely what we imagined. He lost his appetite for the life he had dreamed of in his youth.

The version of himself who had needed fame would have envied the man he had become. Yet now... Johnny no longer wanted to be completed by anyone. He needed to be met.

He knew he did not need a woman to heal him. He wanted a woman whose depth could sit beside his own. They would be two lives running parallel and choosing each other freely.

This would not be out of fear or lack... but out of recognition. They would complement each other. Johnny knew such a meeting could not be forced or hunted... yes.

It would arrive only when recognition replaced appetite and the illusion of lack dissolved. He understood then that what he carried was the elixir earned through loss. It was meant to steady another without rescue.

He would remain available without reaching and present without seeking. A man and a woman who did not seek completion in each other were powerful. They would possess the quiet power of two lives that naturally complemented one another.

This was the meeting of two storms rather than a plea for rescue. He stayed single as an honest choice rather than a performance of strength. There were many opportunities and invitations.

He did not fill his bed or his time. He had seen what happens when men and women use each other as bandages. He refused to turn another human being into a distraction.

He walked and swam and thought and wrote. He let his heart grow quieter instead of harder. Solitude became the forge that made him whole.

Years after the coma... his agent came to him with a proposal. They wanted him on an international tour for his new book... a psychological romance. It explored longing and awakening and the meeting of two storms.

The Rare Flower. He hesitated because part of him wanted to stay hidden near the ocean. Another part of him knew that his story no longer belonged only to him.

Influence is a responsibility. He agreed on his own terms. He would show up fully present but would not let the spotlight own him.

He would sign books and look people in the eye. He would remember that adoration is a passing weather pattern... not a home. He walked into each city with calm steps and a firm spine.

He knew that he could return to solitude at any time and that knowledge made him free. His autonomy was non-negotiable. Now... as he moved through the evening streets... he felt the alignment of a life rebuilt.

The boy who could not read had become the man whose words helped others. The cadet had become the man who walked to his own rhythm. The husband who tried too hard had become the man who knew love must choose itself.

The thread of his life now formed a coherent line of purpose. He paused at a corner watching the light change and the faces passing. Taxi horns sounded in the distance.

A couple laughed outside a bar. Somewhere above him a window glowed in soft yellow. He felt no envy... only a firm openness.

Somewhere in this world... he knew... there were souls whose depths matched his own. Maybe he would meet one and maybe he would not. His worth did not hang on the answer.

Still... a faint intuitive knowing whispered that his path was moving toward someone. Johnny turned and kept walking. His hands were in his pockets and his breath was firm.

His gaze was solid and clear. He did not try to escape his past and he did not cling to it. He carried it like a well-worn coat that no longer dictated where he went.

He was not searching for himself anymore. He had found himself in hospital rooms and lonely dormitories and on foreign beaches. He was a man shaped by solitude... not shattered by it.

The night around him thickened into a soft... dark blue. Storefronts closed and streetlights flickered on. He felt the city's pulse shift from resolution to something more reflective.

In that quiet... one final truth rose in him. A man becomes rare the moment he stops asking the world to define him. He begins living from what he already knows to be true.

Yes... this was the life he had chosen. It was a life anchored in inner certainty. His step carried purpose without display.

The world does not flatter such men... it adjusts to them. Johnny had earned the right to be unmoved. He walked on as a man who had found his way out by telling the truth to himself first.

Somewhere people were reading his words and feeling less alone. Somewhere a woman might be tracing a sentence of his with her fingertips. He did not chase that thought.

He let it pass through him like a quiet blessing. Something inside him sensed that her arrival was already in motion. Manhattan opened before him... wide and alive and indifferent.

Johnny felt no need to conquer it. He only needed to walk through it as he was now. Whole. Awake. Firm.

His life had been put back together more than once... yet something inside had stayed intact. That was the part that guided his steps now. It would recognize the moment another soul stepped into his life.

And when that moment came... he would not fear it. He would meet it. He would welcome it.

Until then... the night was enough. His own company was enough. The long road had been honest... and honesty was the one thing he refused to live without.

He turned down another street and disappeared into the city's lights. He was not lost and not searching. He was moving forward as a man who chose never to go back.

Quiet Storm did not know that a man was walking through Manhattan with her spirit already in his chest. She did not know that every step he took carried the weight of a life prepared for her. Yet somewhere beneath her breasts... and low between her inner thighs... her body had already begun to answer.

As the realization of their shared destiny anchored him... Johnny unconsciously placed his **hand over his heart**. He felt the pulse of the alignment lock into place. Then... he **rubbed his forearm** with a slow... grounded motion and chose to **detach** from the city's noise... letting the universe finish what it had started.

The universe was moving them toward each other with a patience older than time. Both of their souls were already leaning forward to meet what had been written. The knowing settled lower than belief... yes.

It was in the place where breath becomes decision. Some recognitions do not announce themselves as longing or hope. They arrive as quiet alignment... firm... patient... yes... destined.

And once felt... yes... permanently... they do not reverse.

CHAPTER EIGHT

Why This Story Must Be Told Now...
Johnny's Private Journal Entry

I avoided writing this story for most of my life. Clarity lived in the belief that the past was better buried and sealed where it could not be found. Once I told myself the timing was never right... I hoped the truth would not speak back.

Now the truth is final and I could not stand before the boy I once was. Guided by endurance... he did not fade with time or heal into something else. Reality was such that he remained intact beneath every version of the man I became and waited without complaint.

Underneath it all... I am that boy... and this story exists because some truths do not decay. Everything about them refuses to dissolve with time or resolve themselves quietly. Now they wait... and when they are finally spoken... they are not spoken for relief but for reckoning.

Coming forward... healing is not the aim but truth is. Everything presses forward the way an old injury aches before a storm... refusing silence. It has followed me for most of my life and something has been demanding acknowledgment.

I resisted it at first... then less... then not at all. Yes... this is the moment. This is the time to speak what I have carried since I was eleven.

Robert Land Academy was the beginning of a story I never chose. I was a boy labeled dyslexic by a system that did not know how to teach a boy who learned differently. The solution offered by adults was simple... send him away and let structure correct whatever they believed was wrong.

I look back now and see how young I truly was because eleven is the age when a child still believes the world can be trusted. It is an age when disappointment cuts deeper than it should because the heart has not yet formed its armor. I was not prepared for what waited on those school grounds... the isolation... the sudden removal of every softness I had known.

No child ever is. What I understand now is that survival is not born from strength. Survival is born from meaning and a quiet refusal to surrender the belief that one's story is not finished.

Something inside me held that belief long before I knew what to name it. It carried me through those four years and it carries me still as I write these words. The world around us is fractured in ways that remind me of my childhood.

Boys and men are struggling to make sense of themselves and many feel misplaced in a world that demands hardness while offering little space for the parts that feel. I recognize the confusion because it shaped me before I knew how to name it. I see echoes everywhere.

This is why I must write this now. Not for confession and not for sympathy. I write because truth has weight and unspoken truth grows heavier with time.

My story is only one lens yet within it lives the cost of forcing boys into molds that never considered their inner lives. Writing this does not bring relief... it exposes. It tells the truth.

Each sentence asks me to reopen a door I learned to seal in order to live. Restraint has always been my protection and my strength. Telling the truth costs me that protection.

It costs the distance I built to stay functional. I accept the cost now... because carrying it silently has begun to weigh more than speaking ever will. There is no anger left in me as I write these pages.

Only witness remains. Only the slow rise of memories I once tucked away because I feared what they might reveal. Age allows a man to meet his younger self without judgment and to speak for the boy who had no words.

So this becomes the beginning. It becomes the moment I step back into the story I avoided for decades. It becomes the moment I accept that telling it is no longer optional.

It is responsibility and it is respect for the boys who walked those same halls and never found their way back. It is respect for the boy I was... the boy who endured... the boy who believed his life still held meaning. Yes... he deserves his place here.

Before I arrived at RLA I already knew the world did not match the words adults used to describe it. I sensed things long before people spoke them. I saw tension in faces when voices remained calm and I felt currents moving beneath conversations that claimed nothing was wrong.

A child knows far more than adults assume. There was an early loneliness that came from seeing what others pretended not to notice. It is the loneliness of a child who realizes his real questions are never the ones being answered.

I learned to protect the small inner world where things made sense even when the outside world did not. Observation became instinct. Being labeled dyslexic carried an unspoken message in those days.

It allowed adults to believe my mind had failed them rather than consider they had failed me. The label followed me into every room and narrowed the expectations around me. Yes... it pushed me inward long before I knew inwardness would become the ground I would stand on.

My parents believed military structure would fix what both society and the school system labeled broken. They trusted an institution more than the intuition of a boy who felt the world in ways he could not explain. I do not blame them now because they were doing what parents back then thought was right.

They did not know the cost. By the time I stepped onto the grounds in the Niagara Region I already understood silence. I understood that adults listened for confirmation of their beliefs rather than the truth a child carried.

I understood that if I needed to protect the living parts inside me I would need to do it quietly... patiently... instinctively. These early understandings shaped the boy who entered those gates. They allowed me to sense the emotional temperature of a room in seconds.

I learned to recognize the difference between authority that guided and authority that needed control. They allowed me to feel danger even when no one spoke a word. These instincts were not gifts... they were necessities.

They were survival skills. Nothing in my childhood suggested ease... it suggested watchfulness. It suggested caution and it suggested reflection.

Adults often felt unpredictable and disconnected from what was real. That gap shaped me. It taught me to gather truth from what was not said and to trust intuition above surface level instruction.

Yes... it was the beginning of the man I became. The boy who entered RLA was not unformed. He carried years of seeing and listening.

He carried an awareness older than his age and a quiet understanding that if he did not protect himself no one else would. This understanding became the doorway into everything that followed. I remember the air the day I arrived.

It felt heavier than anything I had known and even at eleven I sensed I was crossing into a place that would not return me unchanged. A boy can feel when life shifts beneath him. I felt it the moment my feet touched that soil.

From a distance the Academy looked orderly. Up close... beneath its neat exterior... it concealed a far harsher reality. There was no softness in the voices of the adults. None.

The boys carried tension in their faces the way prisoners carry time. Yes... my instincts knew before the first day began. This was not a school. This was a system built on force.

It was built on crude external power designed to break compliance into the body. And beneath that... something colder still. A silent war where only one truth survived.

Real power was not given. It was not taught. It was seized internally... through absolute command of one's response to inhuman conditions.

Those who learned this endured. Those who did not... disappeared. There was no transition. There was no orientation.

There was no kindness to comfort a child. The rhythm of the Academy snapped around us and expected full submission. The loss was quiet yet devastating.

It was the moment a child realizes he is no longer allowed to be a child. I observed everything. I watched boys try to hide fear behind hardened faces. I watched others attempt invisibility.

I watched staff enforce structure with something colder than duty. For an eleven-year-old who already felt uncertain this place became a level five maximum security prison with no refuge. Something awakened in me that first day.

Not strength... but awareness. A hard awareness arrived that understood I would have to know more than what was shown. I would have to read tone... posture... silence.

I would have to see what others worked to keep hidden. These skills were never offered or optional. They were required. Yes... they had to be learned.

They were not taught. They were extracted... or you did not survive. The structure consumed every hour. There was no margin for an eleven-year-old to miss home.

No space existed to ask why he had been sent away. Childhood was erased and replaced with drill... repetition... exhaustion... and yes... punishment calibrated to break resistance. Strength meant survival.

Humanity was identified... isolated... and treated as weakness. Yet each night before sleep something anchored me. Beds were aligned in rows.

Air was dense with fatigue. Boys breathed shallow because rest required a safety none of us possessed. I stared at the ceiling as the day replayed itself inside me.

Fear pressed against my chest. And still... something did not yield. Yes... something held. Something that could not be confiscated was my self-respect.

I kept the quiet respect I reserved for those who remained kind and good. Every institution carries two sets of rules. There are the visible ones and the real ones.

The real ones lived beneath the surface and dictated who broke... who bent... and who survived. I learned them slowly at first... then all at once. Obedience alone meant nothing.

A boy needed instinct. He needed to sense danger before it arrived and read intention before a word was spoken. The boys taught each other because no one else cared to.

The hidden rules were our real education. Some staff carried authority. Some carried unresolved anger. Some carried a darkness we could feel before we could name.

We learned which voices meant danger and which footsteps meant run. We learned by watching the boys who were punished hardest. Their wounds became warnings.

The hidden rules shaped us. They taught us to move without drawing attention. They taught us to shrink our inner worlds to keep them safe.

They taught us how to survive a place that had no interest in who we truly were. Looking back... I see how these instincts followed me into adulthood. I still read rooms before I enter them.

I still sense the undercurrent of a conversation before a word is spoken. I still measure intent quietly... privately... almost automatically. These habits began as survival and evolved into understanding.

The Academy believed it was shaping boys into strong men. What it shaped instead were children who learned to protect themselves at all costs. Children who sensed danger in silence.

They were children who carried the weight of power long before they understood their own worth. As I write this I feel a strange closeness to the boy I once was. He survived with the tools he had.

He learned the rules required to stay alive. He endured hell. It did not take him. He stayed human.

He guarded the parts of himself the system could not break... yes... the parts that cold world could not touch. He is the reason I am still here... yes... the reason this truth can now be spoken. This is why the story must be told now.

Meaning is not given. It is claimed... yes... claimed without permission. The past does not loosen its grip through time or avoidance. It releases only when met with cold... hard... honesty.

The boy I was held his line through storms no child should have survived. The man I am today... yes... exists because of that refusal to break. I owe that boy my voice... and my life.

As the stillness settles over the page... I place my **hand over my heart**. I feel the resonance of that boy's endurance. Then... I **rub my forearm** with a slow... grounded motion and choose to **detach** from the old pain... letting the truth stand on its own.

Some stories do not ask to be told. They wait... yes... until silence weighs more than memory and restraint no longer protects what it once held back. When a truth reaches this point it is no longer private.

It carries weight meant to be shared... not to justify... not to persuade... but to bear witness. And once spoken... it does not return to hiding. Neither cowardice nor evil can hide in the light.

CHAPTER NINE

A Man Who Does Not Chase

Quiet Storm stepped out of her office building with a composed grace that felt thinner than usual. The day had stretched something inside her that she could not hold in place. Clarity lived in the city that moved in its restless rhythm as though every shift in the air brushed against her.

Once the day ended... she felt the deeper part of her awareness she had kept dormant for years beginning to stir. Now she paused at the top of the steps and let the breeze skim across her skin. Guided by a quiet tremor rising behind her breasts... yes... something had begun moving toward a truth she had not invited.

Reality was such that she could no longer escape the pull of what was approaching. Underneath the surface... time slipped... now... t hen... now... then... with a softness that felt older than history itself. Everything about it lived beneath her calm expression and waited to be acknowledged in the fading light.

Now she walked toward the sidewalk with long measured strides that felt borrowed rather than earned. Coming forward... people streamed past her unaware of the unraveling happening beneath her practiced poise. Everything about the moment in the bookstore returned with disarming truth as his presence rose inside her before she had even looked up.

The recognition pressed behind her breasts as though reminding her of something ancient... yes... shifting the structure of her breath once again. At the intersection she stopped under the fading gold light and felt her breath catch in shallow uneven cycles. She tried forcing them deeper the way she had taught herself to do for years.

Yet the emotional weight rising through her spine spoke its own language and refused to be reasoned with. A warmth gathered beneath her blouse and slipped down her back and settled low in her body. It arrived with a softness she had not allowed in years.

She had believed that her most inner places within her body and soul had turned to stone. Now they pulsed quietly with their own rhythm. They insisted on being felt even as she tried to deny it.

Yes... something inside her had awakened... no longer needing permission. She crossed the street with her usual careful dignity yet something in her life had already changed direction. A question rose behind her breasts as she tried to understand why one unplanned moment with a stranger felt more real than years of practiced connection.

The pull tightened again with a quiet certainty she could not push away. It was the kind of shift that does not announce itself because it simply arrives and waits. She did not chase the sensation.

She let it unfold inside her with a fear that was not dread but recognition. A tide rose through her inner structure and gathered the forgotten parts she had abandoned. During the years she survived rather than lived... she had left these parts behind.

It did not demand action because it only revealed what had been dormant. Yes... she walked as a woman crossing into a threshold she secretly longed for. Johnny moved through Midtown with the firm rhythm of a man shaped by silence... not noise.

The day settled into his body with a grounding force that deepened his senses. Every movement around him felt etched in slow deliberate detail. He carried a pace untouched by chaos as he walked with the presence of a man who did not chase.

He moved only when meaning called him. As always... today's meaning was not abstract... yes... it had a pulse. He reached into his coat pocket and brushed the worn spine of his notebook.

The familiar touch carried a quiet promise as intuition rose before words. The moment in the bookstore replayed inside him not as memory but as a shift in the architecture of his inner world. A rising pressure built in his chest as though fate was rearranging the ground beneath him.

Johnny paused at the crosswalk... the red light flickering through mist rising from the street. His gaze passed over the faces moving past him... yet his attention remained tuned inward. He listened at the quiet point where instinct speaks before thought.

He felt her presence... yes... in the rare way a man shaped by hardship learns to sense patterns before they form. When the light changed... he stepped forward as though something unseen had aligned with the rhythm of his stride. He slowed beside a vendor arranging used books.

The faint scent of weathered pages brushed memory with unexpected gentleness. None of the titles called to him... they felt instead like witnesses to something moving beneath his life. A slow current rose from the base of his spine... expanded through his chest... yes.

It arrived with quiet insistence... as though meaning was approaching on its own terms. He stood still and let the presence arrive. Quiet Storm stepped into the boutique market near her apartment... hoping simple rituals might anchor her.

Yet even the aisles felt altered tonight... as though they carried an undercurrent that mirrored the awakening. She reached for berries... and the familiar gesture drew a tightening warmth behind her breasts. It startled her with its honesty.

Her breath wavered in soft... unsteady cycles... revealing a truth she had tried long to bury. She drifted toward the flowers... drawn by something deeper than choice. Her eyes moved across the colors until they stopped on a single white tulip.

It was standing slightly apart in quiet defiance. The sight settled into her breasts with a tenderness that held her breath. It was calling forward a part of herself she had long kept in shadow.

She lifted the tulip with instinctive care... yes... answering a question she had never allowed to be spoken. She moved toward the exit with a composure that no longer matched what moved inside her. The cool night air greeted her with a lucidness that made the truth rise through her spine.

Something in her life had turned toward a direction she had avoided for years and she felt the shift like a distant bell. The recognition moved through her like a soft ache... yes. It was uniting what she longed for with what she feared.

Three blocks away Johnny approached a small open-air florist glowing beneath warm light. Dozens of flowers filled the space yet he passed over all of them with quiet certainty and deep calm. His eyes stopped on a single white tulip near the corner.

It held itself in silence the way truth holds shape when a man becomes ready to see it. A soft pressure touched his chest as he reached for it... yes. He purchased the tulip and stepped into the night with a steadiness that felt ancient.

The flower rested lightly in his hand yet the moment carried a depth that stirred the ground beneath him. A slow warmth moved upward through his chest and expanded through his breath until his thoughts grew still. Her body answered... yes.

Fate sometimes speaks gently yet it never speaks without meaning. At nearly the same moment... in the same city... two lives reached for the same symbol. They did not know the other had been drawn to do the same.

Their inner worlds moved like twin currents... shaped by an unseen gravitational pull. Two trajectories bent quietly toward a single point... even though neither could yet see it. Quiet Storm felt another tightening rise behind her breasts as she walked home... yes.

Johnny felt the same weight settle beneath his ribs. Quiet Storm entered her apartment with a calm that trembled at the edges... yes... a stillness that did not quite settle. The day had peeled back the surface of a life she no longer recognized.

The air inside her home revealed how much she had hidden from herself. She placed the tulip in a glass and watched the last light touch its petals... linger... then give way to darkness. A warmth gathered beneath her blouse and rose behind her breasts... yes.

It arrived in a slow rhythmic expansion that revealed a vulnerability she had not allowed in years. She ate in silence... emotions shifting like tides she could no longer command. Each breath carried fragments of something returning to life.

She felt a firm pulse moving through her inner world... soft... insistent... with a tenderness she had denied. Yes... something inside her had stepped forward... and refused to retreat. Johnny placed the tulip beside his notebook in the quiet of his hotel room.

The stillness wrapped around him... yes... with a truth that settled deep in his chest. He opened the notebook and wrote several lines that arrived from instinct rather than intention. Each word carried the outline of something unfolding just beyond comprehension... yes... already moving.

Quiet Storm stood by her window and looked out over the glowing city. A subtle trembling moved through her breath as the night deepened. Something inside her had awakened fully.

Her body decided... stepping to the front of her awareness... demanding recognition. Her life felt as though it had turned toward a path she had not chosen... yet understood intimately... yes... in her body. Johnny lifted his gaze toward the night sky with the same knowing.

He sensed a quiet brush of her awareness at the edge of his own. It felt like two signals searching through the dark... aligning with invisible precision. Their longing did not overwhelm them because it did not pull... it aligned... yes... it redefined.

The night thickened with a stillness that held the shape of crossing paths. The city breathed around them... carrying a rhythm neither could name... yet both felt without effort. Quiet Storm touched the windowpane.

She felt the cool glass steady the trembling rising through her body. She was not falling... no... she was remembering... yes. She was remembering what it felt like to be alive... yes... to inhabit herself again.

She felt the return of the sensual woman she had locked away and kept silent for far too long. Johnny felt the same pull move through him... a slow tightening beneath his ribs. The city whispered her presence through the quiet space between his breaths.

He did not chase the sensation. He received it... yes... with the steadiness of a man who no longer resists the truth of his path. Something in his life had shifted... and he felt the shift with full awareness.

Tonight they did not see each other. They did not speak and they did not cross the same street. And yet... the distance between them closed.

Something ancient... unnamed... stitched itself through the quiet space between their lives. It pulled them toward a point neither could see... yet both could feel. The city breathed around them... carrying two heartbeats that had already begun learning the rhythm of the other.

As the connection deepened across the distance... Johnny unconsciously placed his **hand over his heart**. He felt the alignment of their separate worlds converging. Then... he **rubbed his forearm** with a slow... grounded motion and chose to **detach** from the city's noise... letting the destiny of the tulip remain sealed.

Yes... recognition... once awakened... refuses to sleep again. And destiny... once it chooses its moment... yes... permanently... does not loosen its hand. Some moments do not announce themselves as turning points.

They arrive quietly... yes... settling into the body before the mind can interfere. And when recognition reaches this depth... it does not ask for pursuit or permission. It waits... patient... until the path naturally bends toward what has already been chosen.

CHAPTER TEN

The Surrender She Tried to Resist

Quiet Storm opened her eyes before her alarm sounded and felt the stillness in the room press softly into her awareness. Clarity arrived as her breath deepened in a way she did not choose. Once her body answered with a slow pull rising from her inner pelvis... a faint memory stirred beneath her blouse.

Now truth often gathered before thought had the chance to interfere. Guided by a force outside of time... warmth collected behind her breasts. Reality was such that it settled... yes... an echo of the ache that had carried her through the night.

Underneath the pale morning light... she blinked slowly and let the vision form at the edges. Everything felt rearranged inside her body and she sensed it in the tender draw moving through her inner thighs. Now she sat up and placed her feet gently on the floor while her hands rested on her thighs.

Coming forward... she grounded herself against what moved upward through her breasts. Everything expanded with a truth she no longer knew how to quiet. She moved through her morning rituals with practiced precision even as her body refused to return to its old patterns.

The shower ran warm across her shoulders and she felt every drop move along her spine with more awareness than she expected. She dressed without intention and made her coffee while the quiet ache beneath her breasts pulsed in rhythm with her heartbeat... yes. It was pulling her attention inward again.

Each step she took reminded her that something had awakened in her body and refused to settle. She stood by the counter and looked out over the skyline as Manhattan began to wake. Cars drifted along distant roads and lights flickered out in towers that had glowed through the night.

Yet none of it felt separate from her inner world as though the city itself breathed with the same shift. The feeling was moving behind her breasts. She inhaled and felt the tremor deepen through her pelvis... bringing with it the memory of the moment she had seen him.

She sat at her small kitchen table and tried to focus on the structure of her day. Meetings waited and deadlines waited and responsibilities waited. Yet her body drifted toward the moment in the bookstore as though drawn by a thread she could not sever.

Her fingertips brushed the smooth surface of the table and her breath tightened. She felt again the presence she had tried not to name. She set her coffee aside and pressed her palms gently together.

The truth rose inside her with a softness she could not ignore and it felt older than longing. It did not come to her as fantasy... it came to her as recognition. She closed her eyes and allowed that recognition to settle through her breasts... yes.

It was reshaping her morning with a pull she had never expected. Johnny woke before the sun reached the buildings across from his hotel window. As always... he lay still for several breaths and let the weight of quiet settle around him.

He felt the truth he had known all his life. His breath moved through his chest in a measured rhythm that carried the imprint of yesterday. Something in him felt centered... firm... and aligned without effort.

He sat up with intention and placed his feet on the floor while the memory of the bookstore rose. He remembered the instant her breath shifted. He remembered the tremor she tried to contain.

He felt again the rare alignment that had formed between them and he knew better than to dismiss it. His breath deepened as that recognition settled inside him. He moved to the window and placed one hand on the glass.

The morning light painted faint patterns across the buildings and he felt something inside his chest respond. It arrived with quiet inevitability. He trusted the sensation completely.

It had guided him through every turning point in his life. Yes... this was direction rather than coincidence. Johnny prepared his tea with the same deliberate calm that shaped all of his movements.

He wrapped his hands around the warm cup and watched the steam rise. It was as though the vapor was revealing something he already understood. His thoughts settled without force and his body accepted that something new had entered his path.

He opened his notebook and let his pen move without intention while the lines took shape from instinct. When he closed the notebook his breath expanded again. He felt the pull beneath his ribs that had followed him and he did not question it.

His steps carried the quiet certainty of a man shaped by alignment rather than doubt. Something had chosen him already. He walked toward the day with that truth resting in the center of his chest.

Quiet Storm stepped onto the sidewalk and felt the morning air touch her skin with startling truth. The coolness brushed beneath her blouse and rose behind her breasts before gathering low in her middle. She inhaled sharply and felt the ache from the night before return.

It followed her down the steps and through the street... yes. It followed her with the persistence of a truth she could not outrun. She moved with her usual confidence yet everything felt slightly removed.

It was as though her body walked through one world while her awareness drifted in another. People passed beside her without touching the ache rising through her breasts. The sensation moved down through her pubic bone.

She steadied her breath and continued walking even as her inner world refused to quiet. The ache did not fade... it grew more defined with every step. She stood on the subway platform with her hands clasped in front of her.

A tremor gathered inside her inner thighs and she felt her body react as though remembering. She closed her eyes and felt the shift move through her again like an invisible thread. When she opened her eyes her composure felt thinner than she needed.

She could not reclaim the distance she once held with ease. The train arrived and she stepped into the car... holding the rail while the motion pulled her forward. Her reflection appeared faintly on the darkened window.

She studied the woman staring back at her. The calm exterior remained but beneath it she saw something she had tried to deny. Recognition had touched her and awakened a softness she had kept hidden.

The train slowed and she stepped into the building where she worked. The elevator doors closed and the confined space made the ache rising through her breasts feel sharper. She pressed her hand beneath her collarbone.

She felt her pulse moving with a new rhythm. When the doors opened she stepped out with the posture of a woman who intended to function. Her inner world continued to tremble.

She greeted her assistant with a composed smile and walked into her office. She sat at her desk and opened her laptop yet the words on the screen blurred immediately. Quiet Storm's mind drifted back to Johnny Meadows.

She imagined the way he would embrace her symbolic tulip. She remembered the quiet steadiness he carried in his body. She remembered the shift in the air the moment their awareness touched.

Her breath wavered and she pressed her fingertips to her lips. She closed her laptop and leaned back in her chair while the ache deepened inside her breasts. She inhaled slowly and let the truth rise from her lower body.

It arrived with a softness that unsettled her. Something had awakened and something had recognized him. Her body already knew... something had begun moving through her body long before her mind could name it.

She lowered her gaze and felt the warmth gather deeper... yes... undeniable in its pull. Johnny stepped into the morning air and felt the coolness settle across his skin. It carried the quiet authority of something already decided.

He walked with the grounded rhythm of a man whose inner world had aligned itself. The memory of the bookstore rose again as he moved down the street. He felt the pull beneath his ribs deepen with unhurried certainty.

Yes... he knew the feeling of a beginning that had already taken root. He entered a café and ordered breakfast while the quiet murmur of conversation drifted around him. He sat by the window and wrapped his hands around the warm cup.

He was anchoring the awareness forming in his chest. He let the memory of her breath shifting rise through him again with the accuracy of a truth. He did not seek to escape it.

Something in his life had opened and he accepted it without resistance or question. When he stepped back onto the street his stride carried the ease of a man who did not chase. He moved only with what was aligned with him.

His awareness remained centered and he allowed the subtle pull in his chest to guide the rhythm of his breath. The city moved with its usual stress yet he passed through it without absorbing its noise. He trusted the quiet inside him because recognition had never misled him.

Yes... this was the beginning. Quiet Storm spent the next hour trying to force her mind into the shape of work yet every attempt dissolved. She wrote emails she never sent and reread messages she could not comprehend.

She adjusted the position of her body in her chair but the ache behind her breasts persisted. It deepened until her breath trembled. A soft pulse moved through her entire body and she crossed her legs tightly.

She was trying to reclaim authority over her awareness. She stood and walked to the window... resting her hand against the cool surface. The city below her moved in firm motion yet she felt removed from it.

Her breath touched the glass in a faint fog and she pressed her forehead there. She hoped the coolness could quiet the rising ache inside her body. She closed her eyes and felt her pulse move in slow waves behind her breasts.

The pulse moved downward straight up through the center of her lower body. Now... then... now... then... Again... and again... now. Her resistance softened... yes.

She felt her awareness slipping deeper. Quiet Storm returned to her desk and opened her journal. The blank page greeted her like an untouched confession waiting for the courage of truth.

She placed the tip of the pen against the page and wrote a single line. Then she wrote another and another. Each sentence curved toward him and carried the quiet gravity she had tried to silence.

Her handwriting softened and she felt her breath deepen as she wrote what she would never say aloud. She closed the journal and placed her hand gently over the cover. Her breath trembled.

Her awareness narrowed to the warm pull gathering low in her middle. Quiet Storm whispered to herself that something was happening significant within her. She felt the truth settle into her bones with unshakeable certainty.

Nothing in her morning had returned to normal. Everything felt rearranged and everything felt touched by the moment she had seen him. Yes... she knew her inner world had shifted.

Johnny walked several blocks before stopping at a quiet intersection. The light changed and people crossed yet he remained still. He felt the shift inside him again and allowed it to settle beneath his ribs.

It arrived with the calm inevitability that had followed him since dawn. He closed his eyes briefly and let the sensation ground him. When he opened them the world felt clearer.

He stepped forward with the quiet conviction of a man who understood. Quiet Storm returned home hours later and the moment she closed the door her breath caught. She placed her hand over her heart and felt her pulse thrum.

As the realization of her surrender centered her... Quiet Storm placed her **hand over her heart**. She felt the pulse of the truth she could no longer deny. Then... she **rubbed her forearm** with a slow... grounded motion and chose to **detach** from her old fears... letting the transformation complete itself.

She felt the thrum beneath her palm as though answering a truth she could not quiet. She walked into her bedroom and sat on the edge of the bed. Her awareness dropped into her body with a depth that startled her.

The warmth rose behind her breasts and moved downward through her inner-most feminine. She inhaled sharply. Yes... her resistance crumbled.

She lay back and closed her eyes while the moment in the bookstore rose again with full truth. She felt the air shift and her breath change. She felt the recognition her body had surrendered to.

Her body had yielded before her mind understood what was

happening. She pressed her thighs together and allowed the warmth to move through her. Her voice barely rose when she whispered that she did not know what this was.

She only knew she felt it. She placed her hand lightly on her lower body and let the truth rise through her being. She did not push it away.

Something had begun and she felt it shaping her from within. She felt it rearranging the architecture of her inner world with a language older than thought. Her breath deepened as she surrendered to what she could no longer resist.

Johnny turned off the lamp and let the room fall into darkness. He lay on his back and felt the quiet settle around him with the weight of something he trusted. His breath deepened and the sensation beneath his ribs expanded.

This was a certainty that did not need explanation. He felt her presence in the space between thought and breath. Yes... the recognition moved through him again.

She understood it then with quiet truth. This was no longer a moment she could observe from a distance. Something in Quiet Storm had already surrendered.

She had yielded before she decided whether she would follow through. The recognition had moved too deep to be dismissed. It moved too precisely to be misunderstood.

Whatever waited ahead would not arrive as surprise. It would arrive as consequence. Yes... permanently... it would arrive as destiny... her destiny.

CHAPTER ELEVEN

A Voice That Found
Her Again

Quiet Storm sat at her desk with New York City stretching far below her office window. The morning light reflected off the glass towers and scattered across her workspace in soft fractured patterns. Clarity arrived as time softened... and she tried to draw her mind into the focus she relied on.

Once she reached for them... her thoughts slipped away immediately. Now something in her breasts tightened with a low heat that moved downward through the center of her body. Guided by this pull... it gathered between her inner thighs as a reminder that her body had not returned to its former sleep.

Reality demanded she lift her posture and force her attention back to the page. Underneath the words... heat rose beneath her blouse and expanded behind her breasts with soft pressure. Everything brushed across the tips of her nipples until they tingled with restless awareness.

Now her breath deepened in response and dropped lower into her body in an unintended rhythm. Coming forward... the moment in the bookstore rose again with the same undeniable weight. Everything about his presence had entered her nervous system before she even named it.

She pressed her fingers into the armrests as if she could hold herself in place against her own awakening. She stood and moved toward the large window across the room. Each step was controlled on the surface while something unfastened beneath her clothes.

She placed her palm against the cool glass and watched the city shift far below. She told herself she still had control and that this would pass soon. Yet the quiet ache rising along her inner legs answered with its own truth.

Her knees felt unfirm and her ankles light as if she were standing at the edge of something unnamed. She had already opened in ways she could no longer close. She walked back to her desk with deliberate elegance and contained posture.

She opened the file again and tried to re-enter the mental sharpness she was known for. The words scattered the moment her eyes touched them... dissolving into nothing but shapes on a screen. She closed the file and set it aside with a slow exhale.

Her breath trembled at the top of her chest and then dropped again into the swirling heat beneath her blouse. She lowered her head and allowed a single truth to rise. Her body was responding to something she did not seek... but felt more strongly than she could think.

Quiet Storm folded her hands and rested them across the center of her body just below her navel. She felt a subtle tightening pull inward that startled her with its calling. It felt like recognition... not of him alone... but of a part of herself she had pushed into exile.

She lifted her gaze toward the skyline and let the inner truth settle. Something inside her had been called awake that refused to return to sleep. Yes... she no longer belonged entirely to the life she had built.

Johnny stepped into the publisher's lobby with a firm presence that moved ahead of him. People turned subtly in his direction without knowing why... sensing a man who walked by inner compass. His stride held the calm certainty of someone who had spent a lifetime listening to what moved beneath the surface.

He greeted the staff with quiet sincerity and allowed himself to be guided toward the conference room. Beneath his composed exterior he felt a low current rising through the center of his chest. He entered the meeting with unforced authority.

Discussions of projections and international rights for his next novel filled the room. Charts shifted across the screen and numbers moved like a language of their own. Johnny spoke when needed... his tone firm... unhurried... and precise.

Yet his awareness stayed anchored to a deeper thread. The same quiet pull that had entered his body in the bookstore hummed beneath the conversation. He knew that feeling and had learned the difference between distraction and alignment.

This was alignment. Voices flowed around the table while his thoughts moved inward. He remembered the shift in her breath when she first looked up.

He remembered the subtle tremor she tried to hide in her posture. He remembered how the air between them had thickened with meaning neither spoke aloud. The memory pressed gently into his chest like a wordless vow.

Yes... something had begun. He understood enough of his own life to refuse to treat it as coincidence. When the meeting ended he stepped into the hallway and rested his hand against the window frame.

Sunlight touched his knuckles and traced a soft glow across his skin. He felt no agitation and no rush to act... only direction. He allowed that direction to settle deeper into his body.

He let it root itself in the center of his awareness the way truth always did when it arrived without noise. He did not chase the moment. He waited for the moment to reveal his next stage.

He stepped into the elevator with the same grounded stride. People hurried around him in a blur of stress and divided attention while he remained still inside his own resonance. Johnny felt her somewhere in the quiet space beneath his breath.

It was not as fantasy or longing... but as a presence that had taken its place without permission. The sensation was familiar and almost ancient... a signal he trusted more than any plan. Yes... he could feel the invisible thread tightening.

Quiet Storm stepped out of her late morning meeting with her folders pressed tightly against her breasts. Her colleagues spoke beside her about numbers and deliverables and timelines. Their voices sounded distant and blurred at the edges.

She moved down the hallway with practiced confidence... her heels precise against polished floors. Yet a subtle tremor traveled down her spine and warmed the center of her body with startling force. Heat spread behind her breasts and a tingling electricity brushed across her nipples beneath her blouse.

Her breath caught as her body remembered him. Quiet Storm reached the wall at the end of the hallway and let her back rest against it. Her breath deepened and drew inward through her breasts in a quiet surrender.

The folders pressed into her stern line as warmth rolled downward between her hips and along the length of her inner thighs. A soft pull gathered behind her knees and made them feel less firm. She exhaled and closed her eyes for a moment.

Her body already knew it was trying to regain the center she used to trust. She could not. Something significant had taken hold of Quiet Storm from within.

She walked into her office and closed the door with softness. The latch clicked and the sensation inside her body softened into a slow inward draw. She moved toward the window and touched the cool glass.

She anchored her fingertips while everything beneath her clothes trembled. The city moved below her in indifferent motion... yet she felt as if she were standing behind a version of herself that no longer fit. The woman who had built this life felt close and far away.

Her hand drifted up and rested over the upper curve of her breasts. Her heartbeat pressed against her palm with quiet urgency. She remembered the shape of his presence in the bookstore.

He held the space around him as if it belonged to no one and yet welcomed everything true. She remembered how her breath had shifted before she even understood why. She felt all of it again now with deeper resonance.

Yes... she had been found by something she did not know how to refuse. Johnny stepped out of the building and into the sunlight with a firm breath. The rhythm of the city pressed around him in a distant echo of horns and sirens.

None of it touched his internal pace. He moved with the same quiet gravity he had carried his entire life. His awareness remained anchored to the presence that had settled into him.

A subtle warmth gathered in his chest as he crossed the street. This recognition was expanding through him like a calm tide. He entered a café and approached the counter with unforced ease.

His order was simple and the barista met his eyes with relaxed openness. He accepted the warm cup and chose a seat near the window. He wrapped his hands around the warm cup and let the heat move slowly into his palms and up his forearms.

His breath stayed firm as he allowed the memory of her to rise again without resistance. He opened his notebook and let the pen move in deliberate strokes. He wrote about the moment in the bookstore and the subtle pressure that had shifted something deep inside.

Johnny wrote about recognition as a kind of direction rather than desire. It was a signal from the universe that did not chase yet did not retreat. He wrote about the invisible thread that appears between two people without warning.

It feels less like a beginning and more like remembering a path that has been there all along. His handwriting remained even while a low current moved through the center of his body. He paused and let silence fill the space around him.

He rested one hand flat on the page and closed his eyes for a breath. His thoughts drifted to the quiet tremor he had sensed in her. He saw how her composure had cracked to reveal the true woman beneath.

He felt the same tremor in himself now... though it arrived as calm certainty. He lifted the cup and took a slow sip. Yes... something had begun in a way that felt older than choice.

Quiet Storm returned to her desk and sat slowly as though lowering herself into a different version of her life. She placed her folders on the side of the desk and folded her hands together. Her breath rose high in her chest before sliding downward again into a warmth.

The heat spread behind her breasts and drew inward through the center of her body. She felt it gather there with a depth she had not allowed for years. A soft pulse traveled along her inner thighs and into the back of her knees.

The sensation deepened the ache she was trying to ignore. She lifted her gaze to the skyline and traced the line of the horizon. Her thoughts drifted toward him again by pull rather than effort.

She remembered the gentle steadiness of his posture and the way his stillness had steadied something fragile inside. He had unfastened her guard. She felt the memory press against her awareness with a weight she could not soften.

Now... then... now... then... Again... and again... now. He had touched something deep in her that had been dormant and patient and waiting. She pressed her fingertips lightly against the center of her body just below her navel.

She was trying to calm the sensation rising there. A subtle trembling answered her touch and moved upward through her breasts. It brushed along her collarbone and up into the delicate skin beneath her earlobes.

A faint tingling ran along the curve of her lips as if her body remembered the outline of a kiss. She wished now that it had happened. Quiet Storm had spent years cultivating the life she lived.

One unscripted moment with him had rearranged her entire life without force. She rose from her chair and walked to the window again. The cool glass grounded her fingers while heat continued to move under her clothes.

She felt the ache deepen along her inner thighs and she drew her knees closer together without thought. Her breath wavered before settling into a softer slower frequency. She closed her eyes and let the inner truth approach.

She needed to feel his presence again... not his hands or his mouth... but the way the air changed when he stepped into a room. Johnny closed his notebook and placed it beside his tea. He leaned back in his chair and rested his hands loosely on the table.

His posture stayed relaxed yet his awareness sharpened. He sensed the direction of the day with unmistakable weight. He did not know the details and did not need them.

He only knew that something in his life had turned toward a new path. He stood and stepped out of the café with the quiet conviction of a man who followed inner truth. The street stretched before him in long lines of moving traffic.

He walked with firm strides... letting the noise of the city fade to a distant hum. His breath deepened as the sensation in the center of his chest expanded into a calm unwavering pull. Yes... the day carried meaning.

He allowed that meaning to drop further into his body. It settled in the space that had always spoken to him when his life was about to change. Quiet Storm returned to her chair and sat upright with measured posture.

She placed her hand lightly across the upper curve of her breasts and felt her heartbeat shift beneath her fingers. She felt exposed in a way that frightened her and steadied her at the same time. She closed her eyes as a soft warmth slid downward through the center of her body.

The heat gathered with slow insistence between her hips. Her inner thighs tightened and released in small waves that left her breath uneven. She whispered a truth she had tried to resist.

Something inside her had surrendered. She opened her eyes and looked at the stack of work waiting for her. Quiet Storm lifted a client legal file and set it down again.

She inhaled carefully... yet her breath caught at the top and fell once more into the same heat behind her breasts. Her body was answering something she could not plan or schedule. Her awareness narrowed around the memory of his voice.

She remembered the sound and the steadiness of it. A single word from him sounded like it had been weighed before it was spoken. Johnny's echo lived inside her now.

She leaned back in her chair and let her head rest gently against the cushion. Her breath softened and drifted low inside her breasts. She felt warmth move down the length of her inner thighs again with a pull she could not deny.

Her fingers relaxed in her lap and her shoulders loosened as the inner truth she feared settled deeper. Yes... she needed to see him again. Not to fill a loneliness... but because something in her knew she would not be the same.

Johnny walked through the afternoon air with quiet purpose. He did not rush and did not hesitate... simply following the subtle direction rising inside him. His breath moved steadily through his chest as a grounded certainty formed.

Light shifted between the buildings and spilled across the pavement in broken lines. He felt the alignment take shape with an order he trusted more than any map. Yes... he knew her presence would cross his path again.

Johnny turned a corner and let the city move around him without entering his inner space. People stepped aside without knowing why... sensing a man who did not leak his energy outward. His awareness stayed fixed on the quiet thread connecting him to something unseen.

He did not force the day toward a planned outcome... he allowed the day to arrive. Fate did not need his help to orchestrate what was already set in motion. Quiet Storm placed both hands across the center of her body and closed her eyes.

Her awareness dropped inward with surprising ease as though the walls she had built had thinned overnight. She felt warmth behind her breasts rise toward her collarbone and then fall again with soft rhythmic pressure. It sent tingles along the back of her neck.

Her ear lobes grew warm and her lips tingled. Her inner thighs tightened in a gentle pulse she could not explain away. She touched the edge of the truth she had been avoiding.

She felt claimed by a presence that had not yet touched her skin. Yes... she felt found. Yes... she felt Johnny Meadows deep inside her.

She opened her eyes slowly and one clear thought rose through the swirl. The day was no longer hers alone. Something had entered her life and changed its direction without asking permission.

She could fight it or deny it or pour herself into work. Yet she felt the truth gather inside her with each breath she took. She whispered the acknowledgment to herself with quiet reverence.

Yes... she needed for herself to find him again. Johnny walked toward the edge of Rockefeller Plaza with the quiet certainty of a man who knew he was where he needed to be. His breath deepened and a subtle pressure expanded in the center of his chest.

As the realization of his destination anchored him... Johnny unconsciously placed his **hand over his heart**. He felt the pulse of the alignment lock into place. Then... he **rubbed his forearm** with a slow... grounded motion and chose to **detach** from the city's noise... letting the destiny of the meeting reveal itself.

He looked out across the passing crowd with sharpened awareness and anchored presence. He felt her in the air the way a tuned instrument feels the first note. Yes... the thread between them had been pulled tighter.

Neither of them moved toward the other yet because they did not need to. Something had already begun rearranging the ground beneath their lives with quiet synchronicities. The recognition no longer asked to be felt... it demanded to be answered.

It could not be undone. Whatever came next would not arrive as chance. It would arrive as meeting... yes... it would arrive as destiny.

CHAPTER TWELVE

Recognition Without Touch

Johnny stepped out of the café into the firm afternoon air. Clarity lived in his presence as it moved through the street with the calm weight of a man who shaped space. Once he began to walk... his breath rested low and firm... grounded... intentional.

Now the hum of synchronicity threaded through him with quiet certainty. Guided by subtle currents... life spoke to him through alignment and shifts in the inner field that did not go away. Reality was such that he felt one of those shifts now as he walked toward Central Park.

Underneath the stone archway... the noise of the city softened as if it respected his arrival. Every leaf stirred above him like a quiet recognition while he rested his hands in his coat pockets. Now he allowed the memory of the bookstore to rise without effort... the instant she lifted her eyes.

Coming forward... he remembered the break in her breath and the tremor in her posture. Everything about the moment was not about chasing attraction... it was recognition... yes. Recognition always signaled direction for a man like Johnny.

He paused near a bench and looked out across the open space. His awareness gathered inward in deliberate focus while children played in the distance. He listened to the quiet movement inside his chest where the sensation sat like a compass.

It did not argue or explain... existing simply with the certainty of north. He did not rush or push... trusting the moment as it settled here. He allowed alignment to reveal itself... knowing that real crossings announce themselves through sensation.

Johnny sat and placed his hands on his lap with relaxed fingers. He let the truth settle without shaping it. Quiet Storm's presence moved through him again as a firm imprint rather than a memory.

He recognized that the moment had marked him deeply. A path this subtle did not disappear even when life looked unchanged on the surface. When he finally rose from the bench he did not feel unsettled... he felt prepared.

Something was arranging itself gently and deliberately. Direction had already begun its work without urgency. Quiet Storm stood at the edge of her office and folded her arms beneath her breasts.

The gesture felt instinctive and protective and tender. She felt as if she were holding something new and fragile inside her. She stepped toward the window and brushed her fingertips along the cool glass.

The skyline no longer grounded her but mirrored her internal state. It was vast and shifting and full of currents she did not yet understand. She felt them along the backs of her legs and the soft skin under her blouse.

She pressed her palm flat against the glass and closed her eyes. The chill meeting the warmth of her skin moved downward in a slow inward pull. It tightened the space between her hips and sent a faint tremor along her inner thighs.

Recognition was the word her mind finally offered. It was not fantasy or distraction. Something inside her had been touched without her consent.

It awakened in the place behind her breasts she had guarded for years. Her breath trembled as the truth rose higher into her throat. She stepped back from the window and returned to her desk.

She sat slowly and let her hands rest on the armrests. Her reflection appeared faintly in the dark computer screen showing her vulnerability. She saw the softer line of her mouth and the redness at the rims of her eyes.

She saw how her shoulders had dropped from the weight of it. She had built her life around control... yet control had no power here. This feeling warmed the center of her body and refused to recede.

Quiet Storm opened her journal and then stopped. Her breath tightened and her hand hovered above the page. Her gaze drifted until it landed on *The King of Main Street*.

This was Johnny Meadows' first novel that she had read years ago. She lifted it slowly as if touching something alive. Her pulse rose beneath her blouse and fluttered behind her breasts.

She ran her fingertips along the cover as her throat softened. She did not understand why she felt drawn to this book now. Her body reached for it before her mind could intervene.

She opened to a random passage and began to read. The cadence of his sentences moved through her like warm air slipping under fabric. It entered beneath the edges of her blouse and traced a path along her breasts.

His voice on the page entered her awareness with quiet force. It was as if the man with *The Rare Flower* had stepped into her sanctuary. She felt the words settle behind her breasts and drift lower with deliberate heat.

Her breath caught and she pressed her thighs together with an instinct she could not restrain. His written voice touched her deeper than she had prepared for. She read another line and her body answered again.

Heat gathered low and pulled inward through the center of her body. A tingling rose along the soft underside of her breasts. It brushed across her nipples until they tightened beneath her blouse.

Her ear lobes warmed as if catching an unseen whisper. A faint buzzing traced the outline of her lips as though he were close enough to kiss. Her breath thickened and dropped all the way down to her thighs.

The place between her legs began to ache with slow and undeniable awareness. She closed the book gently and held it against herself. She needed a moment to reorient her senses.

The cover pressed into her blouse and the warmth inside her rose to meet it. The contact sent a small shiver along her spine. She whispered to the quiet room asking what was happening to her.

Her voice sounded softer than she remembered. The question did not frighten her but humbled her. For the first time in many years she admitted that something true was moving.

She had not engineered or approved this feeling. Johnny left the park with the firm grace of a man who trusted his inner prompting. Alignment lived in his chest like a warm and grounded current.

He entered the hotel lobby and returned greetings with a calm nod. He moved through the space with stillness. He took the elevator up and unlocked his room without hurry.

Beneath the simple gestures... the bookstore moment pulsed in him. It was a living signal that would not dim. He removed his coat and set it on the chair.

He moved toward the window and watched the city from above. Lights flickered on one by one as the world shifted into evening brightness. He stood in stillness and did not mistake the sensation for vague longing.

It was not yearning but resonance. Two internal worlds were brushing against each other. They were awakening something neither of them had planned.

He felt the inner truth of that with a calm that settled deeper. He sat on the bed and rested his hands on his thighs. His breath deepened as he sensed the inevitability forming.

A quiet pull was drawing two paths into alignment. The next

step would not come from force but from readiness. It would come from the natural unfolding of what had already begun.

He closed his eyes and allowed the stillness inside him to gather. Thoughts fell away until only sensation and truth remained. Something had opened between them and something had begun.

Johnny let himself feel that fully without shrinking it. He simply acknowledged that his life had turned slightly on its axis. He was now walking with a new line running through his awareness.

Johnny remained seated for several minutes in the quiet of his room. The hum of Manhattan pressed softly against the windows. It never disturbed the steadiness in his being.

His breath moved in long and unbroken inhales. Alignment had spoken and he had heard and felt it. He rose and crossed to where his notebook lay.

His fingers rested on the cover for a moment before he opened it. The pen felt familiar between his fingers. The words that came felt like they belonged to a path revealing itself.

He wrote slowly about a woman whose breath changed before she knew why. He described the way her presence shaped the air. He wrote of her posture and the unspoken ache in her gaze.

He recalled the subtle tremor in her mouth when their eyes met. Recognition did not ask for permission but simply arrived. It anchored itself inside two bodies at once.

Each sentence landed with a quiet truth he trusted. He knew these pages marked a new threshold in his story. Johnny closed the notebook and rested his palm on the cover.

He felt the warmth of his own hand linger there. His breath deepened again. He did not know when their paths would cross next.

He knew with certainty that the crossing had already chosen them both. He moved to the window and watched the daylight soften across the city. Somewhere beneath that same sky she was moving through the same current.

Quiet Storm still held *The King of Main Street* against her breasts.

It was the only object in her office that made sense. The weight of the book pressed gently into the ache behind her breasts.

She lowered it slowly to her lap and opened to the beginning. The paper felt cool beneath her fingertips. A subtle warmth slipped down the center of her body.

It gathered between her hips with quiet insistence. Her inner thighs tingled with a soft inward pull. She began to read again from the first chapter.

The younger version of herself had admired the craft and structure. The woman reading them now felt seen. It was as if the words reached back and touched her.

Her breath settled into a slower rhythm with every line. Sensation spread along the curve of her waist. She traced underlined passages with her thumb.

The meaning landed differently inside her now. Phrases about courage and burdens and crossroads pressed into her. He had written into the spaces she never dared to show.

Quiet Storm closed her eyes and let his voice move through her. The cadence of his language carried the same grounded presence from the bookstore. It seemed to move beneath her blouse and across her breasts.

The feeling moved down through her front and into the place between her thighs. Fear and needing touched there. Her breath caught and then deepened as she pulled the book closer.

Her fingers tightened along the spine as a shiver moved up her neck. A thought rose inside her with startling inner truth. She wondered what his presence would do if she moved toward it.

The question sent a soft tremor along her spine and down into her knees. She pressed her legs together and felt the ache between her thighs intensify. It was a clear and honest response.

She did not feel foolish but completely awake. Quiet Storm turned another page and found a paragraph about a man who refused to chase. The description mirrored the stillness she had seen in him.

It was that quiet refusal to perform. She imagined him writing these lines in some quiet room. His hand moved with the same deliberate calm he carried through the world.

The image sent warmth up her throat and into her cheeks. Her body understood the man behind the words. Her guard began to fall in small increments.

It was not a collapse but a soft and deliberate opening. It started behind her breasts and moved outward. She felt parts of herself stretch and breathe.

The narrow band of tension beneath her blouse softened into surrender. Her breathing took on a fuller rhythm. She set the book down and rose from her chair.

She needed air that was not coming from the vents. She crossed the room and stood in front of the window again. The city looked the same yet felt very different.

She pressed her palm against the glass and felt the coolness rush through her. The heat in her lower body held firm. The contrast made her breath tremble.

Something essential had shifted inside her. She turned back to the room and let her gaze rest on the book. She walked toward it slowly... guided by a decision forming beneath thought.

She lifted the book and held it against her breasts. The contact awakened the warmth between her hips even more. A slow pulse moved down the length of her inner thighs.

She understood she was holding evidence of the man who rearranged her. A part of her wanted to resist and return to yesterday. Another part had already stopped fighting and sat quietly.

She imagined him sitting somewhere in the same city. He was unaware that his words were moving through her like this. The thought humbled her and made her lips tingle.

She brought one hand to the hollow of her throat and felt her pulse. She was no longer watching her feelings from a distance. She was in them.

Johnny turned from the window and sat at the small table. He wrote a single line about a woman discovering she had changed. The sentence landed with the unmistakable feeling of inner truth.

He did not need proof. He allowed his awareness to extend outward in his quiet way. He sensed the field around him shift with precision.

Somewhere in that unseen field he felt her presence. Her internal world now resonated with his in a way that could not be undone. He knew recognition had occurred.

Recognition never left the body once it arrived. Johnny closed the notebook and rested both palms flat on its cover. His breath moved with deliberate ease.

He understood the temptation to go searching but held firm. He would not chase. He would allow the alignment to keep revealing itself.

The same thread that brought them together would draw them again. Quiet Storm slipped the book into her bag before leaving. The gesture felt intimate and personal and destined.

She rode the elevator down with strangers while her inner world tilted. Her breath rose and fell while the words echoed within her. She touched the spine of the book and felt the warmth respond.

It was a quiet answer between her hips. Outside... the evening light wrapped around the buildings in gold and silver. She walked toward the subway with measured steps.

Each movement carried the awareness of him. She passed storefronts and faces that blurred around the center of what she felt. Her nervous system had chosen a new point of gravity.

On the train she found a seat and drew the book into her lap. She simply rested her hands on its cover and let the energy move through her. Her thighs pressed together and her breath deepened.

The sensation felt like an opening she had waited for her entire life. When she reached her stop she rose and held the book against her breasts. The simple act was a quiet affirmation.

She was allowing herself to feel and to need. She was allowing her body to tell the truth her mind feared. Johnny prepared for the evening with simplicity.

There was no rush and no performance. He moved through tasks with the awareness that something larger had settled. He straightened the tulip resting near his notebook.

He watched a drop of water trace its way down. The symbol was clear... two lives reaching for meaning without knowing. He sat on the bed and looked at the pages he had written.

He knew they belonged to something he would one day give to the world. He treated that power with reverence and respect. Quiet Storm entered her apartment and placed her keys in the dish.

She exhaled slowly as she slipped out of her shoes. Tension released from her arches and moved up her legs. She walked into the living room and set the book on the table.

The room felt different and more aware. She changed into softer clothes and returned to the sofa. She lifted the book once more and rested it on her thighs.

Warmth gathered between her hips as she let his words wash through her. Each line traced a path through her nervous system. She was connecting mind and body after years of separation.

She admitted her fake pride was gone. Tears gathered unexpectedly at the shock of feeling understood. She let them fall and slide down her cheeks before brushing them away.

She allowed herself to feel what she had spent years bypassing. Her guard was disintegrating. She closed the book and held it against her breasts.

As the stillness settled over her... Quiet Storm placed her **hand over her heart**. She felt the pulse of the story beginning. Then... she **rubbed her forearm** with a slow... grounded motion and chose to **detach** from the city's noise... letting the threshold remain open.

Her breath trembled and then settled into a deeper rhythm. She whispered that she did not know what this was... but she knew it was real. She allowed that word to anchor her deeply.

Johnny lay back and folded his hands behind his head. His eyes drifted closed as his breath synced with his heart. Somewhere a woman was holding his book and letting her guard fall.

He felt the echo in his chest as a warm and firm hum. He surrendered to the stillness and allowed it to cradle him. The day had done its work.

Recognition had deepened and a threshold had been crossed. The next movement would reveal itself in its own time. Until then he would remain ready and grounded.

He was open to the alignment that had already chosen them both. Quiet Storm carried the book to her bedside table. She slipped beneath the covers and turned onto her side.

Her hand rested against the center of her body. She felt the warmth there answer one more time. She closed her eyes and saw his eyes from the bookstore again.

They were present and kind and unmistakably aware. Her body relaxed around the ache. Her guard had fallen because something true recognized her.

The part of her that survived by control had stepped aside. Something more ancient now stood in its place. This was no longer about feeling but about consequence.

Whatever came next would arrive because she was open.

CHAPTER THIRTEEN

The Space Between Heartbeats

Quiet Storm stepped out of her building with her coat drawn close around her shoulders as the first notes of evening settled across Manhattan. Clarity arrived as the city felt sharper at night... with lights shimmering against the pavement and voices blending into a low hum. Once she moved with purpose... people around her faded into a mix of distraction.

Now the city felt different... as if the air itself carried a quiet intensity that matched the unrest moving low through the center of her body. Guided by this shift... Johnny rose before dawn and stood near the window as the faintest hint of morning pressed against the horizon. Reality was such that New York City had softened into its rare quiet state... where the streets held only a few scattered signs of life.

Underneath the slow shifting light... he watched with a calm awareness that settled deeply in his chest. Every breath moved in an even rhythm as the stillness wrapped around him and deepened the pull moving through his entire body. Now... then... now... then... he felt the same inner pull he had carried through the night.

Coming forward... the sensation had intensified into something firm and quietly electric. Everything rested inside him with a truth he no longer questioned. She walked toward her neighborhood café... though she did not feel pulled there for coffee.

She needed movement and a familiar setting where her nervous system could settle long enough for her inner truth to rise clearly. She pushed open the door and stepped inside. The scent of roasted beans and warm pastries usually brought ease to her muscles... yet tonight it only softened the edges of thoughts that continued to press from beneath her blouse.

She sat at her usual table near the window and folded her hands together in her lap. The fabric of her coat brushed the tops of her thighs and she felt a quiet heat gather beneath it... spreading along the soft skin of her inner thighs. Her fingers curled slightly as a tremor of awareness moved from her palms up through her arms and into the tender space behind her breasts.

Her ear lobes tingled as if catching a whisper no one else could hear... yes... as though his voice lived in the air around her. Quiet Storm looked down at her palms and watched them rest there... firm in appearance... while something far less firm moved through her body. She was not a woman prone to impulsive thoughts.

She did not feed fantasy and she approached her life with deliberate focus. Yet the feeling she carried now did not resemble fantasy at all... it resembled truth. It was an internal recognition she had once believed would never come for her in this lifetime.

She blinked slowly and allowed the honesty of that realization to spread through her like warm water under fabric. Heat lifted behind her nipples and pressed gently into the inside of her blouse. It was as if some unseen presence had leaned close enough to breathe across them.

Her lips tingled in response... a sensual faint sensation that made her suddenly aware of her own mouth. Yes... her body was speaking a language she could no longer dismiss. Quiet Storm lifted her gaze to the window and watched the lights blur across the glass.

Her reflection stared back at her with softened eyes and a mouth that looked more open and softened. She saw the quiet conflict beneath her composed expression. The woman who had built her world on restraint was now confronting the limits of her defenses.

She inhaled deeply and felt a tight ache move deep along her inner thighs. The sensation rose from her knees toward the place between her hips where longing and fear met. It was the feeling of needing and being seen.

It felt like awakening. She understood she was standing on the edge of something she could not yet name properly. Her body was already leaning toward it.

She brought one hand to her collarbone and felt her pulse beneath her fingertips. It beat with a slower and deeper rhythm than usual. It carried a quiet insistence that refused to fade.

She let her hand fall slowly back to the table and allowed the full truth to settle inside her without pushing it away. Something had changed within her that she had not invited and could not send back. It felt like an invisible root had sunk itself into the center of her body and would not leave.

She felt with absolute certainty that she was no longer fully in control of the path forming beneath her feet. Yes... the direction now moved through her as much as she moved through it. Quiet Storm left the café and walked slowly down the block with her fingers grazing the edge of her coat.

The cold air brushed against her cheeks and slid beneath the hem of her sleeves... sharpening every sensation. She moved with deliberate steps as if each footfall might firm the shift in her emotions. Yet nothing she did altered the truth forming behind her breasts and between her hips.

Her breaths came evenly at first... then carried a quiet tremor at the edges. She turned onto a quieter street and let the sound of distant traffic fade into the background. The silence made her feel more exposed and more honest at the same time.

She could no longer hide behind the structure of her professional world. Those scaffolds felt thin compared to the warmth sliding along the inside of her inner thighs. Her defenses no longer held the same strength... they felt translucent as if light and feeling could finally pass through the depths of her soul.

She walked with her shoulders drawn slightly inward from instinct... trying to protect a part of herself that had already opened. A subtle warmth moved down the backs of her legs to the curve of her calves and into her ankles. It made each step feel strangely intimate.

Quiet Storm understood on some level that she was not merely reacting to a man. She was reacting to the part of herself that had finally been called forward. Yes... that recognition unsettled and steadied her all at once.

She stopped beneath a streetlamp and placed her hand gently over the center of her breasts... just above where her blouse parted. The warmth of her palm contrasted with the cool air pressing through the fabric. She felt her heartbeat thudding with a deeper rhythm.

The sensation startled her with its honesty. She had spent years believing she could live without this kind of disruption or needing. Yet the recognition she felt in the bookstore had undone something essential she had kept locked away.

She leaned lightly against the cold railing beside her and let her eyes drift across the buildings. City lights reflected against the windows and cast faint shadows along the street. She observed the world with a stillness she rarely allowed herself... feeling each breath move from her breasts down through her middle.

The breath settled between her hips in slow and firm waves. She did not fight the emotion rising inside her but simply allowed it to exist. The ache deep within the center of her body no longer frightened her... it felt necessary.

It felt like the kind of ache that pointed toward something

meaningful. Her inner thighs pulled gently inward and released in quiet pulses that echoed her heartbeat. Yes... her needing felt like direction rather than danger.

She pushed away from the railing and resumed walking. Her steps became slower as the realization continued to settle inside her. She understood that she had crossed an invisible threshold.

Her inner world no longer aligned with the woman she had been two days ago. She felt that difference in the way her blouse rested over her breasts. She felt it in the way the air touched the skin at the back of her neck.

It was as though her defenses and her longing were standing side by side. Each was waiting to see which one Quiet Storm would choose to honor. She exhaled softly and allowed the inner truth to sink deeper into the center of her body.

There was no returning to who she had been before that bookstore. Yes... something had marked her. Her nervous system remembered every detail.

Johnny stepped out of the hotel and walked into the cool night air with an ease that belonged to a man who trusted life. The city around him pulsed with intensity... yet his presence remained grounded and untouched. He carried himself with the quiet confidence of someone who had walked through enough storms.

He did not rush or anticipate... simply following the quiet direction rising within him. He walked along the sidewalk and let the rhythm of his steps match the firm cadence of his breath. His hands brushed lightly against the edges of his coat.

He observed the flow of the city without absorbing its chaos. He felt the subtle pull in his chest that had accompanied him since the afternoon. It rested low and warm as if someone had pressed a hand gently against him from the inside.

It did not feel intrusive but like alignment. Life was placing something within reach that had not been there before. Johnny honored the feeling by allowing it to guide him without force.

He passed storefronts and moving faces without attaching to them. A faint heat gathered behind his firm stern line of buttons and spread through his torso in calm waves. Yes... the sensation felt like recognition continuing to unfold.

Johnny paused near a bookstore display and looked at the reflections in the window. His face appeared calm and firm and composed. He was framed by the warm glow of streetlights that softened his features.

He studied the image with quiet acceptance of the path forming around him. He saw in his own eyes the same stillness he had carried into the bookstore and into his life. He did not question why he felt the shift so strongly.

He understood that some connections do not come from the mind but rise from deeper places in the body. They speak in signals that are impossible to misinterpret. He moved away from the window and continued down the street.

The city noise began to fade as he approached the quieter blocks near the park. The air felt slightly cooler and the sky opened a little more. He let his attention drift inward and felt the lingering memory of her eyes lifting toward him.

He recalled the way her breath had changed in the space of a single heartbeat. He did not interpret the moment as coincidence but treated it with deep reverent respect. Johnny allowed the truth to remain untouched by overthinking.

The recognition he felt belonged to something older than any story he would write. His breath moved in slow and even lines as he walked. Each inhale and exhale deepened the sense of direction resting in the center of his body.

Yes... whatever had begun would reveal itself without his interference. He crossed an intersection and stepped into the faint glow of a streetlamp. The light settled across his well-defined face and down the front of his coat.

He closed his eyes briefly and allowed the night to speak in its quiet way. He understood that the next movement would come without strain. He trusted the unfolding and the universe's timing.

He trusted the instinct rising from the core of his being more than any plan. He opened his eyes and resumed walking with unhurried confidence. He carried the recognition with him as naturally as breath.

Johnny did not need to search... he simply needed to remain available to the synchronicities ahead. The city stretched around him... yet his path felt ordained. An invisible thread was already guiding his steps through the darkness.

Quiet Storm reached the entrance of her building and paused with her hand resting on the cool metal. She did not move right away. Her breath settled into a slow and slightly uneven rhythm.

The echo of her earlier realization returned with greater force. This night had sharpened the truth inside her rather than softened it. It carved out space behind her breasts and between her inner thighs.

Yes... where her deepest needs had always lived. Quiet Storm's most intimate and sexual desires now lived openly. They were permanently imprinting within her body.

Yes... this knowing meant for her the inevitable joining of her soul. She had given herself permission to feel this fated union with her person. Yes... with her true twin flame and soulmate promised before time began.

This was her fated destiny she was wrestling with now. Quiet Storm had the innate knowing deep inside her that their paths were shared. This had been written long ago.

She stood beneath the faint glow of the streetlamp and allowed the awareness to expand through her in a wave. It felt both unsettling and very desirable. Her nipples tingled beneath her blouse as if the cool night air had passed straight through the fabric.

A soft buzz gathered along her lips as though she were remembering the shape of a kiss she had not yet received. She felt the quiet pull inside her as if something had shifted permanently in the center of her body. Yes... as if part of her had already stepped toward him.

She pushed open the door and stepped into the lobby. The warm lighting brushed across her shoulders and softened the intensity she carried. She walked toward the elevator and pressed the button with slow intention.

Her mind attempted to regain its customary composure... yet her body refused to follow. Her pulse carried a deeper beat. Her breath felt slightly caught in her breasts.

Her awareness did not return to the quiet neutrality she once relied upon. Quiet Storm stepped into the elevator and leaned her back against the wall. She let the cool surface firm her through the thin fabric of her coat.

She closed her eyes briefly and felt a tight ache deep along her inner thighs. It felt like an instinctual pull she could not dismiss. She slid one hand lightly along the outside of her thigh.

She felt the muscle tighten and release beneath her touch. It was as if her body were answering a question she had never allowed herself to ask aloud. She knew this sensation.

It was the unmistakable sign that something in her internal world had awakened and would not return to sleep. As the elevator rose she felt each floor pass like a heartbeat. Each small movement sent another soft wave of warmth between her inner thighs and pelvis.

Yes... she understood on a level beyond words that she had already begun to move toward him. The elevator doors opened and she walked down the hallway toward her apartment. Each step felt heavier and more honest than the last.

She turned her key and entered the familiar quiet of her home. She set down her bag and placed her hand on the back of the chair near the entryway. She let some of her weight rest there as the full realization settled.

Quiet Storm could no longer deny it. She felt drawn to him in a way that exceeded logic and the careful walls she had built. The pull did not feel like losing herself... it felt like being called back to a part of herself she had abandoned.

Her shoulders softened as she allowed that truth to move through her. She stood still for a long moment and let the awareness shape itself fully. It felt as if an invisible thread had tightened between them.

As the realization of her internal surrender anchored her... Quiet Storm placed her **hand over her heart**. She felt the pulse of the truth she could no longer deny. Then... she **rubbed her forearm** with a slow... grounded motion and chose to **detach** from the city's noise... letting the fated connection breathe.

The draw did not ask for permission and did not need her agreement. It carried the unmistakable sense of inevitability like a quiet tide that would not turn back. She stood there in the quiet of her apartment and felt the truth sharpen.

This was no longer a question of readiness or restraint. Something had already crossed the space between them and taken root inside her body. The pull Quiet Storm felt did not ask for permission and did not wait for reason.

It simply held its place... steady and truthful and alive. And somewhere beneath the city's noise she knew with absolute certainty. The space between their heartbeats was closing in.

CHAPTER FOURTEEN

The Inner Life the System Could Not Touch...
Johnny's Private Journal Entry

There was a part of me that Robert Land Academy could never touch. Clarity arrived even at eleven... as I felt it living under the surface like a small ember refusing to die. Once the rules pressed down on us with mechanical rhythm... that inner ground stayed untouched.

Now I did not know its meaning... only that something in me refused to surrender. Guided by necessity... the days demanded obedience before thought. Reality was waking before dawn and marching until the cold settled straight into our bones.

Underneath it all... hesitation drew eyes and eyes drew consequences... so every movement sharpened into survival. Every part of the world hardened boys into shapes they did not choose... yet a quiet softness in me held its ground. Now I held it with silent strength... the way a drowning boy might hold his final breath.

Coming from within... that breath lived beneath every command and every punishment. Everything kept the smallest part of me alive when the rest was being shaped into what the Academy demanded. When the Academy pressed too close I disappeared inward.

I learned to firm my gaze on a fixed point and step into a place no adult could reach. It was not escape. It was truth shaped into shelter. That inner room kept the child in me alive when the world insisted he outgrow innocence by force.

It became the only place in my life that belonged entirely to me. No staff member could enter it and no threat could reach it. It held silence that made sense and stillness that did not punish me. It taught me a language beyond fear... a language that whispered how to survive without becoming them.

Every boy created his own survival. Some became stone because numbness felt safe. Some used laughter to keep from collapsing. Some hid their shaking beneath blankets at night.

I survived by watching. I noticed what others overlooked. I tracked danger before it took shape. I read the air the way other boys read books.

Observation became my shield. I could see the tightening of a jaw before a voice hardened. I could sense the cold shift in a room before footsteps approached.

That awareness placed a thin wall between my inner world and a system built to crush softness. It kept me whole in ways the Academy never understood or could take away. Yes... watchfulness became a kind of prayer.

Yes... Silent... Accurate... Grounded. It was the closest thing I had to autonomy and freedom. It taught me that survival begins long before a threat arrives.

It taught me that intuition is not imagination. It is memory trained into instinct and basic human existence. Nights revealed truths no daylight could expose.

Boys pretended nothing was wrong because pretending sometimes held the pieces together. The air carried unspoken fear like a second atmosphere. I lay still and listened to my breath until it steadied into a rhythm I could trust.

Those moments taught me the difference between being controlled and being awake. The dark gave me space to feel what I could not feel during the day. It gave me the first understanding of my own inner life... a life the system wanted to flatten.

It was in that dark that I learned how to stay human. The system took my sleep... my ease... my sense of childhood. It took the softness I once wore without fear.

It did not reach the part of me that remained watchful... composed... and in control. It did not reach the center that refused to harden. Everything the system tried to suppress grew stronger as it pushed against me.

Not loud and not rebellious. I stayed firm as a quiet heartbeat beneath cold ground. That hidden heartbeat taught me to hold my own life close.

I held it even when the world demanded I abandon it. It taught me to remain aware when others numbed themselves. It kept something essential burning.

As the years passed I learned to separate the boy the Academy demanded from the boy I refused to lose. The demanded boy marched... obeyed... endured. The hidden boy felt deeply and questioned the world silently.

He carried compassion that survived where compassion should not have lived. That eleven-year-old boy that was once me lived beneath the surface. He carried more strength than the version the Academy could see.

He became my compass long before I knew what a compass was. He guided my choices and protected my center. He preserved the last part of me that was still a child.

I carried that inward life long after June 1984... when I left the gates of Robert Land Academy. I was fifteen. It shaped the man I became and the way I entered every room.

It taught me to read intention beneath words. It taught me to feel sincerity beneath posture. It taught me to trust truth over appearance.

Retreating inward became both my structure and strength. It became the ground I returned to when the world grew too loud or chaotic. It remained because it had saved me.

It stayed because losing it would have meant losing the child who once refused to break. It became a lifelong companion... whispering a firming presence when life hardened around me. Even now I can feel that inner room the moment I close my eyes.

It has never left. It waits like a firm center beneath noise and distraction. It steadies me when my thoughts drift.

It reminds me that survival is not built on force but on a child's decision to remain human. That inward room carried me through those years. It carries me now.

It carries the boy I once was into the man I had to become. It is one reason this story must be told. The world sees the adult that a man builds but rarely sees the inner ground that kept him alive.

None of us survived that place alone. Each boy carried a hidden history no one asked about. You could see it in the way some boys stared at the floor when staff approached.

You could see it in the way others forced laughter to hide fear. We were children asked to perform adulthood with no understanding of what adulthood meant. Some boys grew loud to mask the cracking inside them.

Some folded inward so deeply that silence became their shield. Some used humor to keep their hearts from breaking. These patterns stitched themselves into boys who should have been playing... not surviving.

I watched these patterns long before I understood them. We learned each other's pain without language. We developed an unspoken system of signals.

A shift in breathing meant someone was close to breaking.

A quick glance meant stay near me. A soft joke meant hold on a little longer.

I read the boys the same way I read the staff. I could sense when someone was slipping. I could feel the weight in a boy's presence even when he faked calm.

Some were collapsing inside their silence. Others hid their fear beneath anger because anger felt safer. Yes... we were children carrying pain without vocabulary.

Our silence was not proof of strength... it was proof of necessity. Speaking truth invited punishment. Vulnerability invited harm.

We buried everything inside tight spaces within our chests. The staff believed they were shaping the men of tomorrow. They did not see the invisible world forming between us.

It was a world of quiet warnings and shared endurance. Small acts of tenderness were hidden beneath rough surfaces. Those gestures saved us more than any adult ever did.

A hand firming a shoulder saved us. A whispered joke in the exact second hope thinned kept us alive. A boy stepping closer to block another from being singled out carried weight.

These were the smallest things... yet they carried weight equal to survival. They were the remnants of humanity. Some boys cracked under pressure.

I remember them with a heaviness that follows me through every decade. The boys who shook at night thinking no one noticed. The boys whose faces emptied during morning formation.

The boys who held their breath when certain staff walked by. Trauma rarely shouts. More often it whispers into the corners of silence until silence becomes its home.

Some boys never found their way out of that silence. Some could not outrun what followed them from those halls. Not all of them reached adulthood.

I learned that slowly through fragments. A name spoken unexpectedly. A message from someone carrying a memory too heavy to hold.

It was a quiet admission of a life cut short without acknowledgment. Their absence is a weight I carry because someone must carry it. Those who survived did not leave untouched.

We grew into men who mistrusted softness because softness once made us targets. We learned to hide fear beneath stillness and silence. We learned to speak little and watch much.

We learned to keep pain close because sharing it never felt safe. These habits shaped our lives long after the Academy lost its grip. They shaped how we moved through the world.

They shaped our relationships and our ability to trust. They shaped the way we breathed through moments that reminded us of childhood. When I look back I see that the boys beside me taught me more about humanity.

They taught me more than any adult there or anywhere. They taught me that courage is often nothing more than standing again after breaking. They taught me that loyalty can grow between individuals who never speak their truth aloud.

They taught me that strength is not domination. Strength is the refusal to become cruel in a place that rewards cruelty. It is the choice to keep compassion alive beneath pressure that should have destroyed it.

Those boys were mirrors. They showed me the parts of myself I did not yet understand. They revealed my fear... my endurance... my tenderness... and my instinct to protect.

They showed me I was not alone in my pain. They showed me that even in silence we are forever bonded to each other. Yes... we are *Brothers of Trauma*.

Yes... they shaped me as deeply as the system that tried to shape us all. They carved truth into my bones that no adult there ever could. They taught me what it means to endure without losing your soul.

They taught me what it means to stay human. As I write this I still see their faces. Some remain vivid while some are softened by time.

All are woven into the same memory. A story built on endurance... on unspoken connection... on innocence forced into early retreat. They were my first brothers.

Brothers were forged in cold mornings and in long nights and in quiet terror. Their weight lives inside me the way memory lives beneath skin. And every time I return to that inward room... the one no system could touch... I find them there.

As the realization of that inner sanctuary anchors me... I unconsciously place my **hand over my heart**. I feel the pulse of the child who stayed human. Then... I **rub my forearm** with a slow... grounded motion and choose to **detach** from the old ghosts... letting the truth stand as it is.

Always present and always waiting. Always part of the story that shaped the man I became.

CHAPTER FIFTEEN

The Man Who Waited

Johnny stepped out onto the balcony and let the night air wash over his face in a slow... grounding sweep. Manhattan glowed beneath him... rising like a field of softened fire into the darkness above. Clarity arrived as he rested both hands on the railing and allowed his awareness to settle into the living frequency below.

Once he stilled... a familiar pull gathered deep in his chest and sank lower through his body in a firm inward draw. Now this sensation had lived inside him since the afternoon... resting beneath his heartbeat like something already chosen. Guided by this truth... he did not confuse the feeling with simple anticipation because it carried the unmistakable weight of alignment.

Reality expanded through his entire body as he inhaled... as though the whole city were exhaling through him in return. Underneath the surface... direction had taken form even if the shape of the moment remained unseen. Everything about waiting had never meant absence for him... it meant restraint guided by respect.

Now he understood that the deepest crossings do not arrive through pursuit but through readiness. Coming from a place of wisdom... what stirred in him now did not ask to be taken but asked to be honored. Everything about his choice was based on the difference between desire that reaches and truth that arrives.

His gaze moved across the distant rows of windows where countless private lives unfolded out of sight. He did not lose himself in those imagined stories because his awareness held firmly to the presence he had sensed in the bookstore. The memory rose without effort and carried with it the shift in her breath and the faint break in her composure.

And... yes... his own body had answered with a quiet recognition that moved from instinct rather than thought. Johnny allowed the moment to live again in his body and to connect to his soul without resistance. Johnny stepped back from the railing and moved toward the small table near the door.

The room behind him sat dim and warm... holding the atmosphere of a space that had listened to many unspoken truths. He sat with a slow calm and placed his hands on the armrests as if anchoring his body to the chair. His breath fell into deeper resonance and each exhale drew the pull inside him into tighter focus.

He closed his eyes and let his attention drift downward into the center of his core. The pull gathered low and expanded outward in slow waves of warmth that moved across his front. His shoulders softened and his jaw loosened as his system opened to the truth rising through him.

The sensation did not ask for control... it asked only to exist and to be experienced fully. He granted it that space without hesitation or resistance. Across the city Quiet Storm stood in her apartment with her hands resting lightly against the kitchen counter.

The familiar hum of evening life moved around her yet none of it settled her because her body felt more awake than the room. A soft ache lived behind her breasts and drifted lower in slow spirals that caught her breath. She lowered her head and let her eyes fall closed so she could listen to the truth she had tried to ignore.

Quiet Storm walked toward the living room and lowered herself onto the couch with deliberate posture. Her back remained straight as if bracing herself against an invisible current moving through her center. Her hands rested neatly on her knees while a faint tremor traveled across her skin in small scattered pulses.

Light from the window painted drifting patterns across her inner thighs and the motion reminded her of the shifting movement inside her. These were two forces crossing... neither fully in her control. Her gaze drifted to the shelf where his book rested in quiet stillness.

The sight of the spine alone sent a thread of heat gliding beneath her breasts and down through her inner loins. Her nipples tightened beneath her blouse with a truth that felt like memory rather than imagination. Her inner thighs grew heavy with awareness and a slow fullness pressed inward in response to the ache.

Yes... her body remembered him. On the balcony Johnny felt a sudden shift radiate upward through his chest and downward through his lower body. It felt as though a distant chord had vibrated into him.

His breath deepened involuntarily and a strong sensation... yes... a tingling rose along his arms before settling in his palms. For a moment he imagined those hands braced around a woman's hips... firm and warm. He was anchoring her while the world faded into background shadow.

He let the image move through him without interruption as if receiving something spoken with meaning. Johnny opened his eyes and returned to the railing with firm steps. The sky had darkened further and the city lights rose to meet it in a deeper glow.

He placed his hands on the cold metal and felt the temperature move into his fingertips. Beneath that surface his blood moved warm and slow while his lower middle tightened in quiet readiness. The pull did not resemble hunger but recognition woven directly into his nervous system.

Quiet Storm rose from her couch and walked toward the bookshelf in slow measured strides. Each step carried a subtle shiver through her knees that felt like surrender to something older than thought. She brushed her fingertips along the spines until she reached his name.

The moment her skin touched the edge of his book a tremor moved up her arm and into her collarbone. It caused her lips to part in a quiet and involuntary breath. She lifted the book in both hands and held it against her breasts.

The weight was pressing into the place where the ache had been gathering all evening. Heat spread outward toward her hips and down between her thighs until her knees pressed together. Her nipples prickled sharply beneath her blouse as if touched by cooled air.

She imagined him behind her with his breath warm at her ear and his chest solid against her back. She felt him kissing her neck and her entire body answered... yes. At that same moment Johnny felt a tightness rise from his middle into his chest.

His breath caught... then dropped deeper as warmth spread across him like a hand pressed gently against his chest. A phantom sensation brushed his earlobe as though another breath hovered there. His legs and chest grew heavier and a strength pooled in his lower body.

Yes... the thread between them tightened again. He stepped inside and closed the balcony door with reverent quiet. Moving to the center of the room he stood tall with his feet grounded and his arms loose.

His breath deepened into his core. His entire body became a listening field as he felt the pull thrumming low inside him with patient intensity. It felt like two inner worlds breathing together across the distance of a universe.

Quiet Storm returned to the couch and lowered herself as though stepping into sacred territory. She placed the book across her inner thighs where the cover pressed against her flesh through the fabric. A shock of heat rose from her knees to her hips and she shifted slightly.

The ache in her body deepened in answer. Her earlobes tingled and the back of her knees warmed as if responding to a voice she had not heard. She opened the book to a familiar passage and let the cadence of his sentences pour through her.

The rhythm slipped beneath her blouse and settled behind her breasts before spiraling lower. Her nipples pulsed gently with each line as though the words themselves carried breath. The ache between her thighs widened into trembling warmth and she swallowed reflexively.

She felt the movement of her throat as if she had taken something intimate into herself. On the other side of Manhattan Johnny drew in a long breath and sat at the table. The pen rested between his fingers the way it had tens of thousands of times before.

Yet tonight the quiet energy inside his hand felt different. It carried weight and charge as if the space between thought and touch had narrowed. When he began to write the sentences formed with a certainty that traveled from his subconscious.

He wrote about a woman who read his words and felt them inside her body as if they were his hands. He wrote about breath slipping across skin and fingertips tracing the soft edge of awakening. He wrote of lips hovering near a place that remembered desire too clearly to deny it.

As the images moved through him a slow warmth rose from his lower front and tightened gently across his chest. He did not rush the sensation but let it move through him with full presence. Quiet Storm read another paragraph and a tear formed at the corner of her eye.

It slid down her cheek in a slow and deliberate line. She caught it with the edge of her tongue without planning the movement. The salt brought her attention fully to her lips... full and warm and slightly parted.

Her breath deepened once more and moved down until it touched the ache gathering between her thighs. She looked at the page but felt him rather than the ink. His presence moved through the cadence of each sentence and settled inside her.

It felt as if her body had opened a door she could not close. Her nipples throbbed beneath her blouse and a subtle tingling rose from her knees to her ankles. She pressed her inner thighs together and exhaled a soft sound that barely existed.

The sound felt like the beginning of something she had not allowed herself to feel in years. Johnny paused and closed his eyes as a ripple passed through him like the drag of a fingertip. Goosebumps rose across his skin and he felt his breath thicken.

The weight of desire settled lower in his body... not as hunger but as destiny. He shifted in the chair and allowed the full gravity of the moment to anchor him deeper. He placed one palm flat over his lower abdomen and felt the warmth strengthen with firm pressure.

Heat climbed from that center up through his chest and lingered at the base of his throat. He allowed the sensation to expand without interruption. He imagined her somewhere holding his book and feeling the same pull.

The thought settled into him with the weight of truth rather than possibility. Quiet Storm opened her eyes and looked down at the page again. She read a line about a man who followed only what aligned with his inner truth.

The description mirrored what she had sensed inside him at their first meeting. She imagined him writing those words alone with his breath moving steadily. His presence was filling the room the way it had filled her nervous system.

Her body answered instantly... yes. Her nipples tightened further... pressing against the fabric with a low ache that deepened each time she inhaled. Heat spread along her inner thighs and the tender skin there prickled.

It felt as if she were remembering a touch she had not yet received. She closed the book and rested her palm on the cover as though resting her hand on this man's chest. Her fingers curled slightly as if they were holding a firm warmth.

She leaned back into the couch cushions and let her head rest against the top. The room felt heavier now... as though the air around her had thickened with quiet electricity. Her breath moved in slow and uneven waves that traced circles through her body.

Now... then... now... then... Again... and again... now. Quiet Storm allowed everything she felt to rise without pushing it away. She let herself need without apology.

She let herself imagine his hands sliding over her hips and his breath near her ear. She imagined his lips brushing the line of her neck and his hands touching her breasts. Quiet Storm imagined him entering her at the base of her inner thighs.

At the same moment Johnny stood and moved back to the balcony door. He did not open it but simply stood in front of the glass. He let the lights of the city pulse against him in quiet resonance.

A subtle tightening moved along his jaw then softened as he exhaled slowly. His desire for her settled deeper within him... not as restlessness but as truth. In him needing created focus and not confusion.

He placed one hand flat against the cold glass and allowed the contrast to sharpen the sensations. Beneath the temperature difference he imagined another palm pressing against his. The image moved through him like a flash of heat and dropped into his groin.

His abdomen tightened and his chest grew heavy with grounded strength. He remained completely still and allowed the energy to flow. Quiet Storm rose from her couch and walked toward the window.

She felt the weight of her own body with each step. She felt the heated heaviness behind her breasts and the tender fullness between her thighs. Her legs felt slightly unfirm as though her desire had moved into her muscles.

She placed her fingertips against the cool glass and stared into the city's scattered lights. She imagined him somewhere in that expanse breathing the same pull and feeling the same ache. She imagined him needing in the same hungry way.

The thought moved through her body like an electric wave starting at her earlobes. It traveled down her throat and across her breasts before settling in her pelvis. Her lips grew warm and heavy.

Her knees softened and she drew them closer together as though firming herself. She was resisting the force of her own awakening. She pressed her forehead gently against the glass and closed her eyes.

The cool surface heightened the warmth beneath her blouse and deepened the ache inside her. The sensation behind her breasts widened and dropped lower in a slow pulsing wave. She breathed out and felt the truth settle deeper into her nervous system.

Yes... she was no longer standing alone. She was connected. Johnny turned from the balcony and walked to the bed with even grounded steps.

He sat and leaned forward with his elbows braced on his knees. He let the quiet gather around him. His breath moved slow and full... carrying the weight of something he no longer questioned.

There was no strategy in him and no impatience. Only readiness for the door life planned to open. He straightened and lay back slowly with his hands resting across his stomach.

As the realization of his path anchored him... Johnny unconsciously placed his **hand over his heart**. He felt the pulse of the alignment lock into place. Then... he **rubbed his forearm** with a slow... grounded motion and chose to **detach** from the city's noise... letting the waiting reach its natural end.

His breath deepened into long firm lines and each exhale drew the pull closer to the surface. He allowed the sensation to anchor him in the space between waking and sleep. It was there that truth often revealed itself and intuition sharpened into direction.

Across the city Quiet Storm stepped back from the window and turned off the light. The room fell into a softer dimness that matched the twilight inside her own awareness. She moved toward the bed and sat on the edge.

For a moment she simply felt the weight of her legs and the warmth between her thighs. She felt the tingling at her lips and her earlobes and her neck... yes. She lowered herself slowly and drew the covers over her nude body.

She placed one hand over her breasts and the other over her center. The heat beneath her palms answered immediately... spreading outward into her hips and loins and inner thighs. She closed her eyes and let the sensations rise.

She no longer pushed away the ache or tried to reason with it. She let it speak to her. Quiet Storm felt his imprint across her body as clearly as if his hands rested there.

He was on her breasts and along the inside of her inner thighs. He was at the back of her knees and at the soft weight of her lips. She inhaled and felt the recognition gather deep inside her.

It was larger than desire... yes... it was primal. It was older than longing. It was the kind of truth the body speaks before the mind can name it.

Across the city Johnny breathed in and out... fully awake inside even as his eyes drifted closed. The pull between them no longer felt like a thread. It felt like a shared field expanding and narrowing with each heartbeat.

Neither knew the other lay in bed with a hand resting over the same places. They were both breathing through the same ache. Yet the connection lived in both their bodies with loud certainty.

Yes... the man who waited was not waiting alone. Yes... something had already crossed this ancient threshold without permission being asked. The connection lived beneath their breaths and inside their nervous systems.

It lived with a certainty that did not flicker or fade. He waited without reaching and she felt without turning away. And yes... somewhere the truth between them held steady... alive... patient... alrea dy shaping the moment when waiting would no longer be possible.

CHAPTER SIXTEEN

A Flower That Chose to Bloom

Johnny rose before dawn and stood near the window as the faintest hint of morning pressed against the horizon. Clarity arrived as New York City softened into its rare quiet state... where the streets held only a few scattered signs of life. Once he watched the slow shifting light... a calm awareness settled deeply in his chest.

Now his breath moved in an even rhythm as the stillness wrapped around him. Guided by the stillness... he felt the inner pull he had carried through the night intensify into something firm and quietly electric. Reality was such that the sensation rested inside him with a truth he no longer questioned.

Underneath his breath... the warm heaviness low in his abdomen lived with quiet focus. Everything about the morning indicated that something had shifted not gently but decisively. Now he moved toward the small table where his notebook waited... sitting with deliberate posture.

Coming from a deeper source... the thoughts that surfaced did not resemble plans or analysis. Everything he wrote resembled knowing that was older than intention and far more exact than logic. He paused... placed the pen beside the notebook... and let his breath settle into the quiet.

Johnny leaned back and rested his hands loosely over his abdomen. He allowed the deeper part of his intuition to rise without pressure. The inner direction forming inside him felt undeniable... even though no external event had shaped it.

He trusted this rhythm because it had guided every meaningful turning in his life. He stood and walked toward the wardrobe with quiet certainty. He chose a simple shirt and jacket with his usual calm decisiveness.

The movements felt intentional yet unhurried... as if the morning itself had expanded to meet him. He lifted the shirt and felt the fabric brush across his knuckles like a subtle affirmation. His intuition guided him with a deep truth.

He did not know why the impulse to step out into the morning felt so grounded and right. He only knew that resisting it would violate the internal compass he lived by. Yes... it settled.

He placed his hand briefly against his chest and felt the firm beat of his heart answer him. The beats carried conviction and direction. It carried quiet inevitability that grew warmer with each passing moment.

The warmth expanded through his chest and anchored itself low in his body. His breath deepened as he stepped toward the door. Johnny moved toward the elevator with the relaxed stillness of a man aligned with his own inner center.

The early hour magnified the silence and filled the air with a sense of expectancy. He pressed the button and waited without tension... as if time itself had slowed to match his pace. His body remained calm and firm.

Without asking permission... he felt the city calling him toward something that had not yet taken form. He did not interpret the sensation as anticipation but as alignment with a direction that had already chosen him. When the doors opened... he stepped inside with his masculine presence.

Quiet Storm opened her eyes before her alarm sounded and stared at the ceiling with a stillness that did not feel like rest. Her body remained warm beneath the blankets... yet her mind drifted into the quiet ache she had carried. She placed one hand over her inner thighs.

She felt the familiar thud of her pulse rise to meet her touch. Her breath caught as the warmth spread through her lower body. Her body already knew the rhythm inside her had changed.

It felt fuller and deeper... as though her body had already accepted a truth her mind continued to resist. She inhaled slowly and let the sensation move through her without interruption. Her body was speaking with a truth her thoughts could not quiet.

She sat on the edge of the bed and let her feet touch the floor with careful intention. She remained still for a moment... waiting for her thoughts to arrange themselves. The feeling inside her did not scatter.

It held its ground with quiet authority and pressed gently against her breasts. She bowed her head and exhaled a long breath. She understood that the moment in the bookstore had marked her in a way she could not reverse.

She rose and walked toward the kitchen with slow... deliberate steps. Each movement felt like a small surrender to what had already taken root inside her. The cool tiles pressed against her bare feet and sharpened her awareness.

She started the kettle and leaned her hip against the counter while the soft hum filled the room. Her thoughts drifted back to the other day with surprising ease. The memory formed in her mind with startling truth.

She remembered the recognition in her breasts when she looked up and saw him. She remembered the sudden stillness that had swept through her body. The memory pressed against her with a density that felt both unsettling and necessary.

Her breath deepened as she steadied herself against the counter. Quiet Storm poured the hot water over the tea leaves and watched the steam rise in soft curls. Her hands wrapped around the cup as if seeking warmth and truth from the same source.

She walked to the window and watched the city beginning to wake beneath her. The morning light painted slow patterns across the glass. Usually this grounded her.

Today it felt distant... as though her inner world no longer matched the external rhythm. She had relied upon that rhythm for stability. She brought the cup to her lips and let the warm liquid settle on her tongue.

A small sigh escaped her as her body softened around the sensation. Her body softened slightly... though the truth inside her remained unwavering. She knew she had crossed an internal threshold that she could not undo.

Quiet Storm felt the tension between fear and longing settle heavily in her breasts. The ache in her body carried a depth she could no longer dismiss. She understood that her life's trajectory had shifted in a single... unannounced moment.

The recognition she felt had slipped past her defenses and taken its place at the center of her being. She could no longer pretend that nothing had changed. The change was shaping her from within.

Quiet Storm stepped into the shower and let the warm water fall over her shoulders in firm lines. She lowered her head and allowed the heat to soften her body. Yes... and then something long dormant awakened quietly inside her.

The water moved across her skin in smooth waves that deepened her breath. She let her hands rest flat against the wall. She breathed slowly and tried to find the familiar sense of control she carried.

The control could not return. The water washed over her

skin... yet something deeper held its place with quiet force. Her body remembered him with divine truth... possession.

Quiet Storm stepped out of the shower and wrapped a towel around herself with slow intention. She walked through the apartment with the softness of a woman moving inside a truth. Her mind traced the memory of the bookstore again.

The memory sharpened rather than faded. Now... then... now.. . then... Again... and again... now... she remembered the stillness. She remembered the intuitive recognition that had moved through her before she could question it.

The memory returned with a depth that felt real in her breasts and lower body. She drew a slow breath. She tightened the towel at her breasts and felt her pulse quicken.

She chose a suit from her closet with the same care she brought to her work. The fabric felt smooth against her fingers as she lifted the hanger. She held the outfit against her frame and studied her reflection.

She saw the softness that had risen to the surface without warning. The softness unsettled her... even as she leaned toward it. Her breath deepened as she felt a quiet longing press against her nipples.

The sensation spread through her body in slow... sensual... forbidden movements. She stared at herself for one long moment and accepted that she had entered a state she could not reason out of. Her heart had stepped ahead of her mind.

Her body recognized him as undeniably real and true. She had accepted it without resistance and the recognition took hold of her completely. The truth of that frightened her and steadied her in the same breath.

She walked toward the window again and looked out over the city. The view felt familiar and distant at the same time. A thin veil seemed to separate her from everything she had built.

The veil had been there before the bookstore. Quiet Storm just had not noticed it before. She whispered a thought she had avoided since she left the store.

She whispered that she needed to see him again. The desire settled inside her with surprising gentleness. Quiet Storm heard an inner voice tell her that this was happening whether she approved or not.

As the realization of her need anchored her... Quiet Storm placed her **hand over her heart**. She felt the pulse of the truth she could no longer deny. Then... she **rubbed her forearm** with a slow... grounded motion and chose to **detach** from her old resistance... letting the bloom complete itself.

She could not reason this away. These feelings were inevitable and written into her body. She was destined to be lived.

She needed the experience of having him deep inside her. As the voice settled... a calm moved through her. She said to herself that something had finally been named.

Something she had always experienced... yet never allowed herself to admit... was here. Yes... something had already chosen to bloom. It lived beneath logic and beyond restraint.

It lived inside the quiet places neither of them could silence anymore. Johnny moved through the morning guided by an inner compass that did not waver. Quiet Storm stood inside a truth her body had accepted before her mind could argue.

And yes... somewhere between those two awakenings... the distance between them thinned. It was not longing or fantasy. It arrived as a living direction that no longer waited to be named.

CHAPTER SEVENTEEN

The Path Only Two Could Walk

Quiet Storm woke before sunrise and lay still beneath her sheets. Early light slipped through the blinds in narrow lines and crossed the walls in soft patterns. Clarity arrived as she stared at the ceiling without moving her hands or shifting her body.

Once she listened to the slow rise and fall of her breath... a quiet weight settled deeper behind her breasts. Now she knew with innate certainty that this had been fated. Guided by this shift... the silence in her apartment felt heavier than usual.

Reality was such that a shift had started inside her and could not be undone. Underneath the surface... her thoughts did not rush forward the way they usually did before dawn. Everything about her body remained very still as heat pulsed faintly beneath her nightgown.

Now she stayed patient and awake while her thoughts hovered between resistance and acceptance. Coming to the truth... Quiet Storm had relied on distance for most of her adult life to protect her from other men. Every part of her realized that distance had kept her intact but alone.

Distance had spared her from disappointment and inconsistency and the quiet erosion that followed every promise. Yet beneath that discipline lived a deeper knowing that this man would not fail her. This was not hope or desire... it was recognition and fate arriving without negotiation.

Yes... distance had been her corner strategy... the place she retreated to when desire asked more than she could survive. Distance had spared her risk and sentenced her to quiet suffering. Now she knew the truth... if she returned to distance she would endure a familiar pain that never healed.

If she surrendered to her true longing she would step into alignment with what had always been meant. There was no safe ground left because her corner strategy had failed her. Destiny had taken its place.

The corner gave her vantage and control. From there she could observe without being drawn in and engage without being exposed. She had stood in that corner with quiet pride and believed she could always return and feel firm.

This morning the corner no longer steadied her in the same way. The slow ache stirring along her inner thighs was answering something she had tried not to name. She turned her head slightly and looked across the room.

Quiet Storm wondered how many times she had used fiction as shelter instead of a mirror. She wondered how often she had hidden behind intellect to avoid admitting her longing for real contact. Without asking permission... the thoughts rose without drama yet carried the weight of years.

A faint tingling moved beneath her skin... uninvited and real. She closed her eyes and released a slow breath through parted lips. Johnny had altered the structure of her inner world by speaking a few well-placed words.

He had entered through one moment of eye contact and the grounded focus of his presence. She felt the truth of that in the soft tightening at her nipples. The answering pulse lower in her body arrived before explanation.

She could not return to her old pattern. That pattern had cracked the moment she looked up in the bookstore. She felt something inside her answer before thought intervened.

She had tried to rely on cool distance again... yet it no longer rose around her the way it once did. It felt thin now and almost transparent. It was like fabric stretched too far to protect what lay beneath... yes... exposed.

Quiet Storm felt vulnerable in a way she had not chosen. She knew this had already been written and already fated. She felt exposed by her own heart more than by anything he had done.

She sat up slowly and placed her feet on the floor. The sheets slid away from her inner thighs. Her body already knew... she stayed there with her elbows resting on her knees.

She felt warmth linger where it could not be ignored. It was steady and present and already accepted. She accepted that her defenses had failed her.

She accepted she could not create emotional space where none existed. She accepted that something in her had opened toward him with a force she had not anticipated. Fear surfaced and softened into a low firm throb of awareness.

It did not ask to be soothed... yes... only acknowledged. She knew she could not outrun what she felt. She knew avoidance would only stretch the ache into a longer and lonelier timeline.

She stood and walked toward the kitchen with careful steps. Her blouse brushed lightly against her skin. Each movement felt like a quiet decision not to retreat all the way back into the corner.

She was chosen and special and unique. Quiet Storm reached for a mug and paused. The stillness of the room pressed around her and sharpened the absence of sound.

Silence had once meant independence and control. This morning it felt like a mirror reflecting her own deep needing back at her. It was settling warmly beneath her clothes and demanding to be acknowledged.

She wrapped her palms around the ceramic and waited for the kettle. When it whistled she poured the water slowly and watched the steam rise in gentle spirals. The ritual usually steadied her and today it only gave her more room to feel.

Warmth traveled through her hands and up her arms. It settled behind her breasts where the ache remained... patient and alive. She stood without moving as truth continued to gather inside her.

She realized she had reached a breaking point without noise or drama. She realized she could no longer live inside the posture of distance she had perfected. Quiet Storm took a slow sip of tea and felt the first quiet rise of courage move through her torso.

It was not loud or reckless but simply real. She moved toward the window and watched Manhattan begin to wake. Lights blinked off in some apartments while others flickered on.

Everything looked familiar... yet her relationship to it felt altered. Her body was leaning forward before her mind had caught up. She was already moving.

For years she had stood at this window feeling separate from the lives unfolding below. From here she could observe without being touched and remain composed. Now something in her needed to step down into the street and risk being seen.

The desire unsettled her even as it drew her forward. It was tightening gently at her nipples... yes... a pull she no longer wished to deny. Quiet Storm arrived at the office later with her posture intact.

Something beneath her blouse carried a fragile pulse she could not settle. She moved through familiar routines with practiced ease and quiet authority. Now... then... now... then... Again... and again... now.

Her body followed the script she knew well while her inner

world drifted outside its lines. Warmth lingered behind her breasts and refused to be dismissed. It was persistent and real.

She closed the door behind her and stood still for a moment. The room felt charged in a way she did not associate with work. Truth pressed upward through her body and held its place.

She reached for her files and opened the first one with automatic accuracy. The words on the page would not stay where she placed them. She tried to pull her focus back into the outer world she had always controlled.

Numbers blurred and logic felt distant. Quiet Storm leaned back in her chair and allowed the fabric of her skirt to draw softly across her inner thighs. The sensation grounded her in a way no calculation could.

The sensation was reminding her where the real movement was happening. She let the silence fill the room and rested her palms on the desk. Her hands had always been firm... even when the rest of her felt tired.

This morning they carried warmth and almost a charge. She knew it did not come from fear. It came from something waking that had waited a long time to be acknowledged.

She rose and walked to the window again. From here the office felt like a structure she had stepped into rather than a life she inhabited. A thin veil separated her from everything she had built.

She had not been conscious that the veil had existed before the bookstore. It had been there before the white tulip and the way his presence had reorganized her inner world. She returned to her desk and sat down slowly.

She closed the file and accepted that discipline would not carry her through the morning. She placed her pen aside and rested her hands in her lap. The low persistent throb of desperately needing him remained deep inside her.

It no longer was asking permission to stay. Yes... it permanently resided in her most sensitive and intimate domain. This knowing had established total and complete dominion over Quiet Storm.

Quiet Storm understood she had reached the place where silence no longer offered peace. Silence now felt like a weight she could not carry forward without an existential cost. The pattern she had relied on had reached its natural end.

Her body and her heart were asking for something closer and truer. She would have to step out of the corner she had mastered. This was her comfort zone.

She left her office and walked the corridor without purpose. She needed movement that did not belong to a task and air that did not ask her to perform. The lights hummed softly overhead and the carpet absorbed the sound of her heels.

With each step she felt the pressure inside her reorganize itself. This was not into resolution... but into resolve. She stepped into the empty conference room and closed the door.

The long table stretched before her in clean deliberate lines. She chose a seat near the center and let her shoulders soften. She rested her palms on the surface and traced the grain beneath her fingertips.

Quiet Storm realized she had been holding her breath without knowing it. She let it go slowly and felt warmth move through her breasts and down into her pelvis. Her longing for him did not weaken her composure.

As the realization of her fated path centered her... Quiet Storm placed her **hand over her heart**. She felt the pulse of the alignment lock into place. Then... she **rubbed her forearm** with a slow... grounded motion and chose to **detach** from her comfort zone... letting the decision settle.

The longing revealed what had been missing beneath her composure. Something could meet her strength without asking her to disappear. Memories rose without invitation of times she had stepped forward and been met with inconsistency.

She had given more than she received and retreated back into distance. The pattern felt old now and heavy. It was no longer aligned with who she was becoming.

Johnny did not belong to that pattern. He had not pursued her or tried to draw her out. He had not asked her to explain herself.

He had simply stood in his own grounded presence. Something in her had moved toward him without effort. This was from a knowing that did not require proof.

She rested her palms on the table and felt steadiness return. She understood that whatever had begun could not be undone by retreat or reason. Her life had already divided quietly into before and after the bookstore.

She rose and left the conference room without rush. The hallway felt narrower than before as if her body had grown more present within it. Each step carried weight and intention.

She felt the pull beneath her breasts and along her inner thighs remain patient and awake. It was guiding her toward the truth telling. She returned to her office and closed the door.

The room felt altered now. She leaned briefly against the door and allowed the tremor and warmth to move together without resistance. She was no longer trying to contain either.

Quiet Storm moved to her desk and sat down slowly. She let her hands rest without reaching for anything. She closed her eyes and allowed fear and desire to settle into a single shared truth.

She did not want to live a half-life anymore. She needed to truly feel what it felt to be joined with another. She wanted to know what soul completion felt like.

When Quiet Storm opened her eyes nothing outside her had changed. The room remained still and her posture remained composed. Yes... permanently... the decision inside her was awake and irreversible.

It did not ask for movement yet and it did not ask for proof. She remained seated and allowed the warmth behind her breasts to deepen. The pulse along her inner thighs stayed present and patient.

It did not urge her forward and it did not allow her to retreat.

It simply held its place... firm and alive and chosen. Quiet Storm understood that courage did not always look like action.

Sometimes it looked like staying exactly where one was while the truth within oneself finished forming. Johnny's number was already there... written inside the cover of the book. He had placed it on an inner page without any instructions or expectations.

She had missed it until now. It was waiting with a quiet gravity she could no longer pretend not to feel. She allowed herself that stillness without judgment.

The choice had already been made within her even if her inner world had not accepted it yet. For the first time in years she did not numb what she felt. She did not hide behind distance or translate desire into something smaller.

She allowed her heart to move ahead of her defenses and trusted that the next step would come when it was meant to. The path before her did not feel safe in the old way... it felt alive. It was a path only two could walk together.

As she remained there with the decision fully formed... she knew the cost of staying silent would soon exceed the cost of speaking. She did not act yet. Quiet Storm simply stayed awake inside herself... ready for what would follow her next.

CHAPTER EIGHTEEN

The Door They Walked Through Together

Quiet Storm approached the wine bar with slow... steady steps. Warm amber light spilled across the sidewalk and gathered around her calves as she neared the entrance. Clarity arrived as she felt the air shift and her breath deepen without permission... pressing softly behind her breasts.

Once her hand rested against her purse... she paused for one quiet moment before stepping inside. Now the interior held candle-light and oak in a low intimate glow. Guided by the scent of wine and warmed wood... her eyes adjusted as she moved forward with quiet intention.

Reality expanded through her pelvis and inner thighs in soft waves... firm and unhurried. Underneath the expectation of feeling overwhelmed... she felt grounded because the room recognized something in her. Everything settled as she drew a slow breath and felt certainty become a calm weight.

Now she saw him sitting at a small table near the back... his posture relaxed and contained. Coming into his gravitational pull... she saw him lift his gaze as if he sensed her arrival. Everything suspended for one long moment as their eyes met across the room.

Quiet Storm felt warmth gather beneath her blouse and tighten subtly at her nipples. Her spine straightened as if her body had been called into alignment. She did not rush... but walked toward him slowly and let each step register through her hips.

Yes... the simple act of crossing the room felt like crossing toward truth. What she understood in that crossing was that return was no longer an option. This was not movement toward a man... but movement away from the woman she could no longer remain.

Yes... something irreversible had already shifted within her. The door was not behind her... it was within her. Once opened... it would never close without cost.

Without asking permission... Johnny rose as she approached. The movement was unrushed and deliberate... not performative or uncertain. He did not smile to persuade... but held still authority in his posture and let it speak.

Quiet Storm felt that authority settle directly on her breasts like a steady and calming hand. He greeted her with a simple hello delivered in a tone that carried weight without force. The sound moved through her like warmth sliding down the back of her neck.

She returned the greeting with a softness she rarely allowed herself to reveal. Her voice surprised her with how easily it came out. He pulled out her chair with quiet calm and assurance.

The gesture was grounded and unobtrusive... as if care was simply the correct thing to do. She sat and placed her hands lightly on the edge of the table... aware of the cool wood against her fingertips. Johnny took his seat across from her with the same calm center she had felt since the bookstore.

The air between them settled into connection that required no effort. The low hum of conversation around them softened into distance. Her body already knew... and Quiet Storm felt the significance of the moment settle deeper with each breath.

Yes... she sensed that something had shifted in her life in a way that would never reverse. She let her shoulders ease and felt warmth spread across her skin. Her breath moved slower now and traveled deeper into her body.

She became aware of a subtle fullness gathering behind her breasts and drifting downward. The sensation was not frantic but firm... steady... and very alive. Johnny watched her with attentive calm that did not crowd her.

His eyes held warmth and restraint... inviting without demanding. He studied her face with a quiet focus that made her feel seen without being exposed. His silence did not ask her to fill it.

A waiter approached with quiet footsteps and greeted them with gentle courtesy. They ordered with simple ease and the waiter stepped back into the dim light. The silence that followed did not feel empty.

Yes... it felt intentional and fated and destined. Quiet Storm allowed her gaze to meet his again and she held it. Longing rose softly within her and moved through her body like a slow tide.

It did not frighten her the way it used to. Yes... it felt like a natural part of her unfolding. She leaned forward by a small measure and let her voice reach him with quiet authenticity.

She told him she had not expected to feel what she felt the moment she saw him. She admitted that something about him had disarmed her in a way she could not explain. She said it plainly... as if stating fact rather than pleading.

Johnny nodded once with slow understanding. He did not rush to comfort her. He held her complete attention and truth with calm respect and let it stand.

Then he responded with equal sincerity. He told her that in the bookstore he had felt her before he saw her. It was a subtle turn inside him... as if something already knew and simply waited for his eyes to catch up.

He admitted he had felt a rare pull he could not ignore. His words were simple... yet they carried undeniable weight. Quiet Storm felt her heartbeat deepen as the truth stretched between them.

It was settling lower into her pelvis like gravity becoming home. The waiter returned with their glasses of wine and placed them gently on the table. Quiet Storm lifted her glass and took a small sip... feeling the warmth move across her mouth.

She set the glass down and let her fingers rest around the stem. She was aware of the contrast between the cool glass and the heat building beneath her blouse. Yes... her breath deepened as her body received the moment.

Johnny remained still... his posture relaxed and contained. He did not reach for his glass right away. He watched her with calm attention and let the space do its work.

His restraint carried direction... and Quiet Storm felt it register along her spine. Quiet Storm then spoke again... her voice softer now. She admitted she did not understand what was happening... yet she did not want to retreat.

The words rose without effort and settled as truth. Yes... the admission sent a slow warmth through her pelvis and into her inner thighs. Johnny leaned forward slightly and held her gaze.

He told her he respected her honesty. His voice was firm and unembellished... offering no reassurance beyond his presence. His simplicity grounded her to the core of her being.

He spoke of sensing depth in her that mirrored parts of his own life. He said alignment and destiny did not need to be rushed. The words landed with quiet authority and not suggestion.

Quiet Storm felt her shoulders ease as if her body recognized leadership through his masculine assurance. Silence followed... thick and alive. She rested her hand lightly against her neck and felt warmth rise beneath her skin.

Yes... the night felt as if it were beginning to mark her in ways she would remember with complete truth. Quiet Storm's posture leaned subtly toward him without any hesitation. Johnny did not move.

He allowed her body to respond first. His stillness held direction and made the space feel safe to enter. Quiet Storm felt that safety settle deeper... yes... lower in her body.

She lifted her chin slightly and met his eyes for a longer moment. Her heartbeat slowed and dropped lower... firm and sure. His gaze expanded her rather than consumed her.

Yes... she felt her inner guard soften without effort. He spoke her name once. The sound traveled down the back of her neck and spread warmth behind her breasts.

He shared with her he had sensed a part of her that had been waiting patiently. The truth of it settled behind her breasts and opened outward. Quiet Storm leaned forward by a small measure and rested one hand closer to the center.

She did not reach for him... she opened. The movement carried surrender rather than pursuit. It was sending heat through her body... then continuing to her hips and into her inner thighs.

Johnny placed his hand on the table with intention. He chose the distance and held it. The warmth radiating from his skin reached her palm without contact.

The space between them thickened immediately. He spoke of fear appearing when something real approaches the heart. His tone did not soothe or persuade... but named an eternal truth.

As the heat between their hands anchored her... Quiet Storm placed her **hand over her heart**. She felt the pulse of her total consent lock into place. Then... she **rubbed her forearm** with a slow... grounded motion and chose to **detach** from her old defenses... letting the crossing complete itself.

Quiet Storm felt her body lean toward the warmth between their hands as if guided by a strong pull. She looked down at the space separating them and felt a soft ache gather low in her body. Yes... her breath caught and released.

When she lifted her eyes again... something inside her had already chosen. Johnny remained still... grounded and patient. His presence felt like a firm hand on the lower curve of her back.

Quiet Storm felt her shoulders lower and her spine lengthen as if aligning itself to him. The moment held. Quiet Storm lowered her gaze again to the space between their hands.

The warmth radiating from him gathered in her palm and traveled slowly up her arm. Yes... sensation pooled behind her breasts and settled deeper into her pelvis with patient insistence. Her body leaned forward by a fraction without thought.

She moved her fingers the smallest amount closer. The motion was barely visible yet unmistakable inside her. Yes... it felt like stepping beyond a line she had guarded for years.

She let her fingertips hover and listened to what her body already knew. Johnny shifted his hand closer with controlled intention. The movement was minimal and decisive... chosen rather than reactive.

He did not hurry... he set the distance and held it. Their fingers rested inches apart. Heat pressed into her palm and spread through her inner thighs in slow waves.

Quiet Storm drew a steady breath and felt her hips soften. Yes... the waiting became active rather than restrained. She lifted her hand and let her fingertips drift forward in a deliberate arc.

When her skin grazed his... a warm pulse moved through her chest and dropped into her lower middle. Her breath caught and released on its own. Their contact was precise and unavoidable.

Johnny turned his hand and enclosed hers with calm strength. The grip was firm and sure... neither tight nor tentative. The containment anchored her immediately.

Heat moved through her shoulders and down her arms as her posture aligned itself to him. Again... and again... now... Quiet Storm leaned naturally into the warmth of his palm. The ache in her inner thighs softened into fullness.

Yes... her body recognized being held without being taken. She felt seen without being claimed. Johnny held her hand without shifting and did not speak.

His stillness carried direction and allowed her to arrive fully. The quiet confirmed the choice she had already made. She lifted her eyes and met his gaze.

What she saw there was not dominance or possession... it was presence. Yes... followed by her willing submission to this man. The reflection steadied her and deepened her resolve to live in this moment.

Quiet Storm felt a quiet surrender settle through her body. This was not really a submission but her total consent. Yes... a yielding that came from recognition rather than need.

Her breath slowed and moved freely. Johnny maintained the same grounded calm that had drawn her from the beginning. He did not pull her closer but allowed her to remain where she was.

She was held and free at the same time. The balance felt exact... settling in Quiet Storm's body. Yes... the door they had walked through together did not announce itself with sound.

It closed softly behind them without locking and without warning. Yes... permanently... what changed was not the room or the night. It was the internal alignment neither of them could step back from without loss of self.

He held her hand with calm intention. She remained present without retreat. And yes... in that quiet balance of holding and choosing... something irreversible settled between them. It was not a promise or possession... but truth now awake and unwilling to return to sleep.

CHAPTER NINETEEN

The Second Surrender

Quiet Storm woke and the very first thought she had was Johnny. The thought arrived before language and settled into her body with quiet weight. Clarity arrived now... then... now... then... finding its place without effort.

Once she lay still... she felt how completely he occupied her inner world. Now the recognition steadied her rather than startled her. Guided by the memory of touching him a thousand times in dreams... her breath carried him forward.

Reality was not something she planned or resisted. Underneath it all... it existed as undeniable truth... yes... and her body had already agreed. Every part of her rolled onto her back and stared at the ceiling as early light pressed through the curtains.

Now the glow traced her collarbone and moved across her softness. Coming forward... her breath deepened and gathered behind her breasts before drifting lower. Everything about the morning indicated she had arrived fully inside the truth as she sat up slowly.

She whispered that she had touched him a thousand times in fantasy. And yes... now... he had touched her in the physical. The words felt ceremonial rather than indulgent. Each memory had left a mark on her body.

Each had drawn her closer to what she already knew. She walked to the mirror and studied her reflection for a long moment. Her eyes carried the weight of the night and beneath it a growing fire.

She remembered his gaze on her... the way it pierced without force and saw without demand. Yes... the memory sent warmth down the back of her neck. She turned her head slightly and felt phantom heat where his hand had rested.

Yes... it settled... sensation gathered at the small of her inner thighs and lingered. She could almost feel his breath near her ear... slow and firm. Her shoulders softened in response.

She turned away and stepped into the shower. Water poured over her skin... hot and unrelenting... tracing her shoulders and breasts. Quiet Storm braced her hands against the tile and tilted her head back.

The rush of water filled the room. The water ran between her breasts and down her front. It moved along her hips and brushed the inside of her inner thighs.

She knew it was only water. Yes... her body did not. Quiet Storm's body remembered him and responded as if his hands were there... firm and sure.

Warmth spread and gathered low without resolution. She breathed through it and allowed the sensation to exist without directing it. When she stepped out of the shower her skin glowed with heat.

Steam clung to her shoulders and drifted upward. She wrapped herself in a towel and stood still for a moment. The quiet felt right through her body.

She walked to her closet and let her fingers trail along the fabric of her clothes. Every choice felt weighted with his presence. She chose something soft and simple... a dress that brushed her knees.

It followed her shape without display. Yes... she felt alive in it. She dressed slowly and noticed fabric against skin.

Without asking permission... she was not dressing for the world.

She was responding to him. Even in his absence she felt the pull to honor what had already claimed her inner world.

Quiet Storm moved through the kitchen and performed the ordinary acts of morning. She reached for a knife and thought of his strength. She lifted her coffee cup and thought of his mouth.

There was no use pretending any longer. She sat at the table with steam rising from her mug. She tried to read but the words slipped away.

Her attention returned to the sensation in her body. She rested her forehead in her hand and smiled softly. She was no longer fighting it.

Each imagined touch had weakened resistance and strengthened truth. Yes... she felt stronger for admitting what was already real. The surrender was calm and very real.

She left her home and walked into the day. Sunlight warmed her shoulders as she moved down the street. Every man she passed blurred into shadow.

Every sound muted except the echo of his voice within her. She was not walking toward errands or obligation. She was walking toward him... yes... even when he was not physically there.

Her body knew direction before destination. At the gym she placed her hands on cool metal and pushed against weight. Her muscles strained and trembled.

With each movement she imagined his presence behind her... firm and guiding. She imagined his hand at her waist... his chest aligned with her back. Her breath deepened and her hips moved with intention.

She remained alone in the room yet not alone within herself. Every repetition brought her closer to the truth she had already crossed. She met friends for lunch and laughed at their stories.

Her smile was genuine and her presence warm. Still... her heart stayed elsewhere. Each voice reminded her of his cadence and each pause of his silence.

Quiet Storm wondered if they could tell she was gone in a way that could not be retrieved. Her body already knew… she wondered if they could see that she already had given herself completely to him. Yes… without question… she already belonged to him.

Yes… the knowing felt ancient and settled deep within her. This certainty did not arrive suddenly. It unfolded as recognition and settled through her body like memory returning.

She believed it had been placed there before time learned language. She had touched him a thousand times in secrecy and shadow. Each time her body opened further.

Each time her authentic soul leaned closer. Each time she said… yes… without speaking a word. She knew now that to fight it would mean loss of self.

The thought clarified rather than frightened her. Her posture straightened as if aligned by truth. The afternoon moved on and she went for a massage.

The therapist pressed into her shoulders and back. Each touch echoed him and drew her deeper into sensation. She closed her eyes and let her receive him like she had a thousand times.

Pressure moved along her spine and into her hips. She breathed heavier and whispered his name beneath her breath. Yes… something unlocked that had been buried for decades.

When she returned home the sun was setting. She lit candles and sat in their glow. The room felt alive with his presence.

She saw him in the chair… in the mirror… in shadow. She walked slowly through the home where she felt she once lived. Each step echoed the truth inside her.

She touched the doorframe and imagined his hands holding her against it. Yes… pressing against her there. She touched the bed and imagined his weight settling on her with total masculine presence.

Quiet Storm lay back and spread her arms. Her body loosened and her breath slowed. She breathed in and whispered his name.

She breathed out and whispered… yes… I am yours. Her thoughts looped through the day and found him everywhere. He was direction... destination... and yes... Quiet Storm's destiny.

This had been fated. There was no longer resistance. Only her total release through her willing submission to this man... yes.

She spoke his name aloud and felt her body answer. She spoke yes and felt her soul answer. She was ready to touch him again... not in dream... but in flesh.

She remained still as candlelight flickered against the walls. The glow traced her shoulders and moved slowly across her curves. Warmth gathered beneath her skin and traveled downward... yes.

It was settling with quiet pleasures. She sat up and let her feet touch the floor. The wood was cool beneath her soles and grounded her.

She rolled her shoulders once and felt sensation move along her spine. Her breath deepened again... invited and honest. She walked to the window and looked out at the evening sky.

The fading light mirrored something closing while something else opened deep within her. She pressed her palm to the glass and imagined his hand covering hers from behind. Yes... the image sent a slow pulse through her hips.

She returned to the center of the room and let her dress brush her thighs. Fabric against skin felt amplified now. Every sensation arrived with deeper meaning.

She sat in the chair and crossed her legs slowly. Awareness drew to her inner thighs and the warmth held there. She closed her eyes and let the feeling rise without directing it.

She thought of Johnny's stillness... not his actions but his presence. The way he did not rush or fill space unnecessarily. Yes... her body responded to restraint more than imagined touch.

Quiet Storm now hungered for Johnny's touch... yes his thrust inside her. She rested her hands on her knees and straightened her posture. Her skin lifted naturally and her shoulders relaxed back.

She felt open rather than exposed. Quiet Storm whispered his name again and the sound settled rather than echoed. Her breath followed it downward and expanded.

She allowed herself to feel how deeply she had already said... yes... to her complete submission. She returned to the bed and sat at its edge. Her hands rested on the fabric and felt the memory of his presence there.

Yes... Quiet Storm remembered his weight and warmth on her body with so much sensual detail. Quiet Storm lay back again and placed one hand over her left breast. Her heartbeat was calm and deliberate.

The other hand rested lower and followed her breath. Now... then... now... then... Again... and again... now. She then found herself moving her other hand further down between her inner thighs.

As the heat of her own touch anchored her... Quiet Storm placed her **hand over her heart**. She felt the pulse of the story beginning its final turn. Then... she **rubbed her forearm** with a slow... grounded motion and chose to **detach** from her old pride... letting the submission complete itself.

Yes... touching her soft inner fold of her pelvis... yes... pleasuring herself. While imagining Johnny... yes... thrusting deep within her. Her thoughts drifted to the future without resolution.

She imagined seeing him again and the calm that would follow contact. The image calmed her rather than stirred fear. A quiet resolve settled through her body.

The second surrender was not dramatic or desperate. Yes... it was chosen by her willingly with absolute truth... calm strength and... yes... total surrender and submission to her darkest desires. Quiet Storm turned her head and watched candlelight play along the wall.

Shadows moved slowly and felt companionable. She was no longer alone with the feeling. She breathed deeply and allowed the moment to close around her.

Sleep approached not as escape but as continuation. The last thought she held was Johnny's presence. Yes... the second surrender did not arrive as collapse or craving.

It arrived as truth. Yes... she did not lose herself in it. She found the part of her that had been waiting quietly beneath discipline... distance... yes... her longing... now satisfied.

Quiet Storm's body rested calm and open. Her breath moved freely without the urge for fight or flight. Yes... permanently... as sleep finally claimed her... the truth remained awake inside her.

It was not asking for permission or speed. It was only asking to be met fully again by him. Yes... her Johnny.

CHAPTER TWENTY

The Ghosts That Followed Us Into Adulthood...
Johnny's Private Journal Entry

Not every boy who left Robert Land Academy made it into adulthood with his life intact. Clarity arrived as I watched some disappear slowly over the years... absorbed into patterns they could not escape. Once they vanished... swallowed by choices shaped before they understood their own pain... they were still with me.

Now these boys became ghosts that follow me even now... their absence holding immense weight. Guided by their memory... I see how the Academy taught us how to endure rather than how to live. Reality meant we stepped into adulthood carrying invisible fractures that looked like strength to others.

Underneath it all... the ghosts moved quietly inside habits of mistrust and bracing for danger. Every part of these adaptations was a way for boys to stay alive in places that did not see them. Now I understand that without meaning... survival becomes a weight that follows a man into every room.

Coming from the silence... I learned about some of the deaths by accident through a message or a name. Every story ended without recognition... without anyone naming the system that shaped their suffering. These were the boys I had marched beside... whose beds once lined up next to mine in the dark.

The ones who survived did not all survive whole... as many carried a heaviness that seeped into everything. Some buried their emotions so deeply they lost the path back to themselves entirely. Some lived with anger that had no clear target... while others drifted through relationships without knowing how to let anyone near.

Childhood trauma does not disappear just because a boy gets taller or older. It grows with him... waiting in the background of his life to step forward when the world grows quiet. What makes these ghosts so persistent is the memory of who we were before those years pressed into us.

I can still feel the younger versions of the boys I knew and the way they tried to be brave. They reached for hope even when it felt thin... yet those earlier selves never had the chance to grow. They froze at the edges of those grounds... standing behind us like shadows that refuse to fade.

There were nights long after I became a man when I woke with my heart racing. Sometimes faces rose back to the surface and sometimes only the feeling did. I see now that these moments were my mind trying to process what it had sealed away to keep me moving.

These ghosts were not there to torment me... but were there to be seen and witnessed. They were meant to be processed and shared with the world. They were waiting for the day I would stop outrunning what I already carried in my chest.

The most painful ghost is the boy I once was... the eleven-year-old who walked through those gates. He learned to hide his softness because softness drew punishment in that place. He stayed alert when he should have been sleeping... watching everything because no one was watching him.

Writing this is the first time I have been willing to sit with him without turning away. Some men avoid their past because they fear what they might uncover in the dark. I avoided mine because I feared confirming what I already knew to be true.

The Academy shaped me in ways I am still discovering... teaching me to stand alone and read danger. It taught me to endure without complaint and to carry wounds in silence. These patterns did not dissolve with time... but waited patient for acknowledgment and peace.

As I write this I feel something shift as the ghosts do not feel as heavy. They feel recognized and named and held in a way that was not possible when I was young. This is why I must write this now... not to tidy the past... but to tell the truth.

I want to bring what has lived in shadow into the open where it can finally breathe. Some of the boys I knew will never have their own books because they are gone or locked away. *Brothers of Trauma* is my simple way of making sure these lost boys are not erased.

Their lives and their suffering mattered... and their absence still matters to me today. Survival is not simply a matter of staying alive... though I did not understand that as a boy. I thought walking away from the Academy would mean leaving it behind... but distance did not separate me.

You carry what shaped you... no matter how far you travel across the world. As the decades passed... I began to face a responsibility I never asked for. The boys who did not make it cannot speak... and those still carrying wounds often keep them buried.

A survivor must bear witness... which sounds simple in a sentence but is not in life. To bear witness is to tell the truth without sanding down the hard edges. I avoided this for most of my life because I lacked the readiness to let the weight move through me.

There comes a point in a man's life when the past stops staying politely in the background. It stands in his way and demands to be seen without the lie of avoidance. I want to leave this world without unfinished truth lodged in my chest.

The responsibility to speak is not about assigning blame... but about deep understanding. We lived inside a system built to shape boys without asking what they were carrying. We learned to survive in ways that cost us pieces of ourselves that we are now reclaiming.

The boys I grew up with were not weak or broken by nature. They were children placed inside an environment that did not understand their inner lives. Their stories are woven into mine whether I speak them or stay silent in the dark.

Writing these words is not easy... as each line asks me to look at years I once ignored. Yet something in me feels steadier now that I am honoring the boy I once was. I have lived long enough to see how discipline without understanding turns into lasting harm.

There is a strange peace in accepting this responsibility as a task that finally fits me. It feels like the completion of a journey I did not choose but must finish. I am writing because I see what those years reveal about how boys are formed and how men struggle.

The Academy was one place... but the forces inside it are not contained by a fence line. The world tells boys to be strong while ignoring the injuries that resilience conceals. It teaches them to silence their pain and then acts surprised when they break later in life.

RLA did not invent these failures... it just made them visible and concentrated. I am writing because truth spoken from a lived life carries weight no abstract argument can match. My story is one example of something happening quietly in many institutions today.

Parents need to know what happens when a child is labeled instead of understood. Teachers need to see what happens when they stop asking how a boy's mind really works. Leaders must recognize the cost of using discipline without emotional ground.

There were boys who broke under the weight of that institution and boys who never came home. Their stories deserve the dignity of being spoken out loud. Silence protects no one and only lets the same harm repeat itself in other forms.

Brothers of Trauma is a light directed at the present rather than the past. It shows how men carry ghosts they never invited into their adult lives. If these pages help one person look at one child differently... then the years were not wasted.

I avoided this story because I thought telling it would reopen rooms I had locked. Now I see that speaking it opens the windows and lets air into spaces closed for too long. It frees the man I am now from pretending those years did not make him.

The purpose is to give voice to boys who were never allowed to speak. We must make it impossible to deny that the cost of silence is higher than the cost of truth. That is why these words must live on the page until I finish.

Even though this story begins in a quiet corner of Canada... the meaning reaches further. The Academy was a concentrated version of a deeper pattern that remains. A boy's inner life is often ignored until the damage starts to show.

As the weight of the ghosts begins to lift through this testimony... Johnny unconsciously places his **hand over his heart**. He feels the pulse of the boys who survived and those who did not. Then... he **rubbed his forearm** with a slow... grounded motion and chose to **detach** from the Niagara soil... letting the truth stand in the light.

Every society builds structures meant to teach discipline and responsibility. The fracture appears when the structure becomes more important than the child standing inside it. A boy learns to harden because hardness is rewarded while softness invites punishment.

RLA made this tension impossible to miss in every inspection and formation. We were shaped by a system that demanded obedience without emotional ground. The result is boys who appear strong while carrying fractures no one sees.

What happened to me at eleven is happening today to boys who grow up under pressure. Some are raised where achievement matters more than well-being. Wounds to children repeat across generations when no one speaks their names.

The Academy taught me that a child's emotional world does not vanish. It waits in the tone he uses with his children and the distance he creates. That is the universal part of this story where pain that is denied does not die.

A child learns whether trust is possible or dangerous based on his early environment. Those lessons walk beside him into every room for the rest of his life. They walked beside me and more individuals than we care to admit.

Healing begins when truth is spoken out loud and silence no longer feels safe. It shows how essential it is for adults to pay attention to inner worlds. If these pages help someone see that... then those years carry meaning.

There has always been a vow running underneath my life since September 1980. I did not have the words then... but I felt a quiet conviction. That conviction never left and grew louder with time.

Achievement and responsibility were layers I used to outrun those early days. The boy who entered at eleven never stopped waiting for the man I am now. Writing these words is me finally returning for him.

The vow was simple... I would not let what happened to us disappear without meaning. I would not allow the world to forget boys who endured more than they should have. I would speak for those who could not speak for themselves.

Telling this story is about reclaiming the past and honoring the children we were. It is about refusing to let our experience be reduced to words like character-building. The truth runs deeper than the narratives used to justify what we were put through.

I carry the memory of boys who never came out whole or never came home. Their stories live with mine and give weight to every sentence on these pages. They are part of the vow because they cannot be here.

I am not writing because I enjoy walking through these sealed buildings. I am writing because silence would mean I accepted what happened as acceptable. I refuse to let it be meaningless.

I will honor the boy I was by refusing to hide from what shaped him. I will honor the boys beside me by refusing to let their suffering disappear. I will search for meaning inside hardship we once carried alone.

This journal is the ground on which *Brothers of Trauma* will stand. It is the truth I owe to the eleven-year-old and the man I have become. I have finally stopped running from the ghosts of my past.

CHAPTER TWENTY-ONE

The Vessel

Quiet Storm sank deeper into the bath... the water lapping against her shoulders... warm enough to blur the edges of thought. Clarity arrived as the water stayed cool enough to keep her tethered to the moment. Once she closed her eyes... the steam clung to the air and softened everything as though the world wished her to let go.

Now in the darkness behind her eyelids... she felt Johnny's presence. Guided by the rhythm of the water... it moved now... then... now... then... as a pulse inside her body. Reality was such that she felt as if the water carried his unseen touch directly into her skin.

Underneath the flickering candlelight along the edge of the tub... each ripple carried more than water. Every movement carried suggestion and invitation as her breath deepened... slow and uneven. Now she wondered if it was hers or his breath that filled the space because Johnny did not need to be here to be felt.

Coming from the current she could not escape... his words still clung to her skin like a directional metronome. Every part of her was firm as she realized needing him had become a truth she could finally hold. The bath became her little sanctuary and the vessel she had dreamed of.

It was the place where the feminine was held and protected and allowed to expand without fear. She could feel herself stretching beyond edges she once kept tight. Without asking permission... with every stretch Johnny's presence pressed closer.

It was not pressure but permission to enter her. She tried to tell herself it was imagination... but imagination had weight when it carried his name. She had learned that the mind could lie... yet the body did not.

Her body had been speaking since their intimate night and it spoke again now. She lifted one hand out of the water and let it hover. Droplets slid down her arm before falling back with a sound too loud in the silence.

Her skin was not empty but brimming with sensation. It was a longing that felt too old to be new and too new to have been there all along. She formed the shape of his name with her lips without sound.

The echo returned to her breasts as though he had answered deep inside her again. Yes... it settled. The water kissed her skin and she thought of his hands.

The thought settled between her shoulder blades and then her inner thighs like a quiet claim. It was as he had been the night he entered her... deep within her... after their dinner. The vessel and the light... she remembered the mystics had called it.

She was the vessel... open and waiting... and he was the light that filled and pressed and expanded in her. The idea frightened her and calmed her at the same time. Safety and false pride and surrender twined around her like the water itself.

She had guarded herself against the word destiny for most of her life. Destiny sounded like something that demanded belief... and she had always preferred control. Yet here it was... rising to the surface uninvited and undeniable.

Destiny was not always stars and prophecy. Sometimes destiny was a current that found two souls and refused to loosen its grip. Sometimes it was the way a woman recognized herself only when a man held her.

He was firm enough for her to soften. Her body already knew... she had stopped trying to swim against it. Yes... she let the water carry her and in that surrender she saw her Johnny.

She imagined his eyes first... firm and knowing. They did not ask but they saw. Then she heard his voice... firm and gentle... threading into corners of her mind she had never allowed anyone to enter.

Then his presence followed... that masculine boundary that made her feel safe and free. It was not submission the way she had feared it in the past. It was release.

It was the kind of release that allowed her to rise while letting herself fall. The paradox made her breath deepen again. Quiet Storm was both the vessel and the current within it.

He was both light and the firm hand that held that light without forcing it. The water cooled against her skin... yet warmth inside her grew. Her head tilted back and wet hair clung to porcelain.

She remembered a question he had asked her. She remembered him asking whether she felt safe and whether she could let herself imagine. And here... in the quiet of her bath... she knew the answer had already been given.

She had imagined and she had let go. She had given him the kind of power that does not come from demand but from deep trust. Yes... that deep trust itself became her desire.

Each ripple against her skin felt like a reminder. Each inhale felt like her response. Her body became fluent in a language she had not studied but somehow always known.

Johnny was not a stranger to this language... he was the dictionary that explained it. Every thought she tried to push away circled back stronger. It was not that she wanted to think of him... but that he lived at the center of her being now.

The bath was no longer only water... it was memory and suggestion. Yes... it was prophecy. Quiet Storm saw them together without forcing the image.

She saw it as inevitability and as a thread tugged from a sacred fabric. It was a sacred promise that had already been woven. Her throat tightened and then softened.

Yes... her breasts rose as though she had been given permission to breathe again. She told herself to stop and to breathe. Now... the n... now... then... Again... and again... now.

The breath carried him deeper into her. The stop became an opening. Fear became a pulse of heat low in her inner loins that reminded her she was alive.

Her lips parted with a breath she did not know she had been holding. She traced the edge of the tub and imagined it was the line of his jaw. She imagined the breadth of his shoulder under her hand.

The fantasy rooted itself deeper... not as escape... but as rehearsal for truth. She let herself drift further in the water as though each breath was a choice. The choice was not to indulge but to stop lying to herself.

Yes... the honesty moved through her like a slow... powerful... unstoppable wave. Her body tightened and softened in cycles she could not control. Warmth gathered behind her breasts and then traveled lower.

As the heat of the water anchored her... Quiet Storm placed her **hand over her heart**. She felt the pulse of the vessel becoming whole. Then... she **rubbed her forearm** with a slow... grounded motion and chose to **detach** from her old armor... letting the light fill the space.

Her inner thighs pressed together slightly and then relaxed. She heard a quiet sound escape her and did not judge it. Johnny became inseparable from her response.

He was not demanding... but he had become the axis her body turned and rested on. She whispered his name again... this time with sound. It lingered in the steam and returned to her like an answer.

She felt claimed... not by force... but by recognition. She felt claimed by her own willing surrender to what was true. This was what she had been circling around her entire life.

It was not competition or compromise... but union. It was a union that did not erase her but expanded her vessel. It was the union of vessel and light.

It was the union of boundary and freedom and the union of seeing and being seen. She allowed herself at last to feel her sensuality without shame. She was a woman who longed to be desired and cherished without being reduced.

In her inner world Johnny was the only man who had ever truly seen her. He did not see her performance or her armor... he saw her. In that recognition hunger awakened... not frantic... but her authentic truth.

She needed more of that gaze and more of that steadiness. She needed more of that calm authority that did not need to announce itself. Her eyes opened to the dim candlelight.

Quiet Storm watched the water surface ripple and wondered what it meant to step beyond fear. It was not for later or tomorrow... but for here. Here nothing existed except the water and the truth moving through her.

She realized she had already taken the plunge. What once had frightened her now stabilized her. Desire no longer threatened to undo her life... it clarified it.

The fear that had kept her guarded for years loosened its grip and would not return. She had already surrendered more than she intended. And yet she did not want to rise back up.

The depth had become the place where she finally felt herself. This for Quiet Storm was a hunger and a deep need. She knew she needed Johnny.

He was not a distraction or a fantasy to manage... but the truth. She needed him as she had never needed any man before. It was not out of weakness... but out of wholeness.

Yes... she needed to give herself completely to the kind of love that held her without consuming her. Quiet Storm drew in a long breath and let it out slowly. The exhale stirred the candle flames and made them tremble.

For the first time in her life she felt no shield around her. It had slipped away and dissolved into the water. What remained was a woman no longer resisting her own longing.

In that truth she admitted what she had circled for so long. She needed him as the answer her body... mind... and spirit had craved her entire life. Quiet Storm let her head sink against the porcelain.

Her eyes closed again. She knew that when she woke tomorrow the imprint on her soul would still be there. She knew she would not be able to shake the image of him... strong and close.

She did not want to. Johnny was within her breath and her thoughts and her heartbeat. He was within her in the way her posture had changed.

He was within her in the way her body no longer argued with itself. Yes... she surrendered to it and discovered it was not weakness. It was repair.

It was the reassembly of a woman who had been divided for too long. What had changed was not the longing but the relationship to it. She no longer felt pulled apart by desire but reorganized by it.

The magic elixir was her bluestone. Now she did not fight it because it had always been Johnny himself. From that moment on Quiet Storm carried with her forward her Johnny.

She carried her ability to remain whole while needing deeply. She felt herself becoming whole through honesty and surrender. She was willing to be held.

The vessel was repaired because she stopped leaking her truth. What healed her was not the man himself... but the moment she stopped abandoning her own knowing. Yes... the repair was internal and irreversible.

She could now need without dissolving and open without disappearing. The vessel did not mend because it was filled... it mended because it learned how to hold. Johnny had never been in search of many.

Johnny had always been in search of his rare flower. And now beneath Quiet Storm was the only audience that mattered to him. She sat up slightly and let water slide down her shoulders.

She watched it run over her collarbone and over her breasts. The water disappeared beneath the surface. The motion felt like cleansing and claiming at the same time.

Her breath steadied. She understood now what his masculine presence truly was. She also understood what her feminine presence had become.

She could move through the outer world composed and sovereign while remaining open to sensation. Yes... permanently... it was not control over her. It was Johnny's containment that let her expand.

It was his direction that made surrender safe. Quiet Storm rose from the bath slowly and stepped onto the mat. Cool air met her skin and lifted goosebumps along her arms and legs.

She wrapped a towel around herself and held it tight at her breasts. Yes... she felt tender but not fragile. She was free for perhaps the first time in her life.

She walked to the mirror and met her own gaze. The world would meet her differently now because she no longer abandoned herself. Her presence carried a quiet gravity that did not seek approval.

She had crossed the ordeal and conquered and returned. Her eyes were clear. Her face looked softer without losing strength. She saw a woman who had stopped negotiating with her own longing.

She whispered his name one more time... quietly. It was not a plea but a fact. The sound settled in her breasts like a vow.

She turned off the bathroom light and walked toward her bed. Candlelight from the other room reached her in faint bands. She moved with a calmness she had never known.

She lay down and let her body rest. Quiet Storm's breath slowed. Her mind quieted. The vessel held.

Nothing was leaking anymore and nothing was chasing. Her journey had closed its circle and she stood inside it whole. In that holding she understood that this was where love was born.

One last time... Quiet Storm sighed his name... Johnny Meadows.

Sneak Peek of
The Rare Flower Sequel

You are still here because something in you is not yet finished. Clarity arrived before thought formed... yes... the pressure in your chest that lingered after the final page. Once you felt the presence of a man who stands in his truth without flinching... you were marked.

Now a connection like that does not dissolve but settles beneath the surface of your breath. Guided by this resonance... it waits and then rises again with quiet insistence. Reality exists in the now... th en... now... then... yes... it remains.

Underneath the words... this is why you kept reading until the very end. Every part of you knows there is a power only a complete man carries. Now it is not spoken but felt... yes... before it is understood.

Coming from a place of calm certainty... Johnny carries that power into your awareness. Everything Quiet Storm feels... you feel too... long before you allow the truth to reach your mind. Otherwise... your breath would not have slowed and your body would not have leaned forward.

You would have stopped here if you weren't already open. What comes next does not offer distance but moves toward you with intention. It arrives with the steadiness of a man who does not retreat from depth or truth.

Johnny does not break under the force of a woman who feels more than she speaks. He meets her intensity with strength and patience and a quiet fire. This fire awakens something you have carried for years without language.

Yes... this is not hesitation... it is inevitability. You asked for more and your body has already agreed to the terms. What follows are two chapters from *The Rare Flower* sequel... *The Queen of the Night*.

As the anticipation of the next story anchors you... Johnny unconsciously places his **hand over his heart**. He feels the pulse of your continued presence. Then... he **rubbed his forearm** with a slow... grounded motion and chose to **detach**... letting the bridge to the sequel remain open.

Read them the way your body already knows how... open... present... awake... and... yes... sensual.

Peter J. Merrick

APPENDIX ONE

The Couch

Quiet Storm did not expect her apartment to hit her the way it did. She walked through the door after her trip and dropped her bags by habit. Clarity arrived for a brief second as she pretended everything was normal.

Once she noticed the still air... the space smelled faintly of her perfume and old flowers. Now on the surface... nothing had changed... yet her eyes fell on the couch. Guided by a sharp twist inside... she had to stop and grip the back of a chair.

Reality was that it was not just a couch but the place where her body had once stopped lying. Underneath her mind's many stories and excuses... her body had no masks. Every part of her remembered what happened there with Johnny in a way that felt immediate.

Now time had folded and brought those nights crashing straight into her chest. Coming closer slowly... she moved as if walking toward a memory that might burn her. Everything about his presence settled her and set her on fire at the same time.

By the time she reached the couch... her heart was pounding hard enough to hear in her ears. Her fingers touched the fabric and her knees almost gave out. It was as if the couch pushed the air from her lungs and replaced it with images.

She saw herself lying back with her hair spread across the cushions and her eyes half desperate. Without asking permission... she saw Johnny leaning over her... calm and focused. She remembered her hands grasping at him and needing more without words.

Her body reacted now as if he were still there. A slow heat rose and moved outward... spreading through her breasts and down her arms. It moved into her thighs as she felt the ache between wanting to run and needing to stay.

Her body already knew that while her pride could argue... her body would not. It told the truth with trembling muscles and shallow breath. She sat down carefully as if she might disturb ghosts.

The cushion gave way under her and it felt too familiar. This was the exact spot where her back had arched beneath him. Now... then ... now... then... Again... and again... now.

This was the place where she had let herself go and surrendered total control in the flesh. She could almost feel his weight above her again... steady... firm... and unshakable. He had held her as if she mattered more than the world outside.

Her mind tried to speak up about risk and timing and old wounds. These were the reasons she recited during her trip to Peru and on flights. The words came... but they had no force against the flood of sensation.

How do you talk yourself out of a memory your whole body insists is sacred? Then the jealousy came... yes. At first it was only a flicker that she pushed away before it formed.

She wondered what if he is not alone on a couch now. What if he is with someone else who reads his chapters and feels what she felt? What if she comes to him and he touches her the way he touched you?

Her chest clenched so hard she pressed a hand there to hold herself together. Quiet Storm saw it in her mind... Johnny sitting on another couch in another room. Another woman was beneath him... learning the rhythm of his breathing.

Another woman was feeling that calm fire in his eyes that once made her feel naked. Images she did not want played against her will. She saw another woman's fingers digging into his shoulders as her head tilted back.

She saw the way he would hold her... firm and present... the way he held Quiet Storm. The scene twisted inside her because it was a threat her mind created. It knew exactly what was at stake.

Her hand moved across the cushion again... slower... searching for proof he had been real. She remembered the sound of her own voice and the way her breath came in broken waves. Sacred words had slipped out as if her soul had taken over her lips.

He did not laugh or mock or pull away. He held her closer as if he understood that her body and spirit had finally agreed. They had agreed on Johnny.

No one else had ever taken her that far back into herself. No one else had been allowed to. The thought of him guiding another woman into that same depth made her stomach churn.

This was not just jealousy over sex... it was jealousy over meaning and being known. If another woman stepped into that sacred space... it would be a space Quiet Storm had walked away from. Her breathing grew rough as she leaned back and let her head touch the backrest.

Closing her eyes did not help because the memories only became sharper. She felt his hand on her hip anchoring her. She felt the slow drag of his fingers along her spine.

She felt the moment her body relaxed fully and trusted him as she had never trusted anyone else. The couch beneath her might as well have been on fire. Every inch held a touch or an uncontrolled moan or a sacred memory.

It was where she crossed a threshold she never thought she would cross. It was where she realized she could not hide and did not want to. The realization that she had chosen to run from that connection cracked her chest.

Quiet Storm's mind flashed another image of Johnny on a different couch in a different city. This woman did not doubt herself or pull away. She did not hide behind excuses but fully surrendered and stayed.

Quiet Storm could almost hear that woman's easy laugh afterward. The woman might curl into him and call him hers. The pain that followed felt real in her body.

It moved slowly through her thighs like something sharp pressing inward. She realized she was not only afraid of Johnny finding another woman. She was afraid of Johnny staying and choosing someone else.

She feared another woman who would not hesitate or doubt what was being offered. Someone would take what Johnny gave and keep it safe without dropping it. That thought hurt more than loss because she was afraid of being replaced.

She was afraid of someone who knew how to hold what she almost lost. She opened her eyes and looked around the room at the curated objects. All of it looked solid and impressive... yet none of it could reach the part of her that was restless.

That part lived on this couch... under his hands... in the sound of her own voice crying out. She understood something with painful truth. With Johnny... her body had finally told the truth.

It told her what her heart had suspected but her mind would not admit. This is your person and your soulmate and your twin flame. This is the man whose presence makes you feel terrified and alive.

She had stepped into that truth and then ran out of it... hoping it would wait. Now the thought that he might not be waiting broke her. Betrayals and distance and years of suppression had never reached this dark place.

The images did not rush but arrived slowly. She understood that she had created them by running. This was not about losing a man... but about turning away from the only moment she was seen.

Nothing was taken... she simply stayed still and erased what had been destined. Quiet Storm leaned forward and pressed her elbows into her knees. Her hands covered her face as the tears slid down slowly and steadily.

She was not crying because Johnny left... but because she saw how she pushed him out. She was crying because her body knew the truth she had betrayed out of fear. The jealousy returned deeper and more focused.

As the realization of her betrayal anchored her... Quiet Storm placed her **hand over her heart**. She felt the pulse of the truth she had tried to run from. Then... she **rubbed her forearm** with a slow... grounded motion and chose to **detach** from her false pride... letting the surrender complete itself.

In her mind... another woman touched the scar on Johnny's eyebrow. Another woman made him laugh and heard him speak in that calm... thoughtful tone. Another woman's body relaxed under his weight.

Another woman saw the same presence that once undid her. Something fierce rose inside her at that thought. It did not come from ego but from recognition.

Yes... permanently... this was her place and she had abandoned it. If another woman laid next to him now... it was her own doing. She inhaled deeply and sat back... letting her hands fall.

The cushion felt like both comfort and accusation. It reminded her that she had tasted something rare. It reminded her that if she lost it forever... it would be because she chose fear.

Her pride tried one last time to bargain about closing this chapter. It promised that time would dull everything... but her body did not accept that bargain. The electric memory of his touch refused to be treated as a casual event.

Quiet Storm let the conflict burn through all excuses. When the fire settled... what remained was simple and heavy. She loved him and she needed him in a way she could not explain.

Her greatest fear was not rejection but that she would never again be known like this. She feared she would spend her life remembering a man she walked away from. The couch sat quietly beneath her holding the imprint of everything shared.

It did not move or argue... existing simply as proof that something real happened. She placed her palm flat on the cushion and whispered a truth into the room. She was speaking to him and to herself.

She had made him unreal so she could step away... but her heart knew better. Johnny was real and what they had touched was real. Only now she realized the one thing she failed to do... she did not go to him.

If she did nothing... she would lose the one doorway into the love she had prayed for. Somewhere in that realization... her pride began to break. It cracked silently under the weight of her deepest fear.

For Quiet Storm... the most terrifying thought was not that Johnny might love someone else. It was that someone else would let him love her fully. Quiet Storm would be left with nothing but the memory of his hands and a couch that remembered everything.

APPENDIX TWO

The Shema

Quiet Storm did not plan to come to San Diego. At least that is what she kept telling herself on the plane while the miles passed. Clarity arrived when she looked out the window and saw the coastline growing closer.

Once her chest tightened in a way she knew too well... her mind tried to say it was only a coincidence. Now her body knew better and understood exactly why she was really coming. Guided by this truth... she realized she had tried for months to drown Johnny out in movement and noise.

Reality was that she had filled her days with superficial friendships and hollow spiritual talk. Underneath the Scrolling and the lonely pictures... his presence found her in her breasts and her stomach. Every part of her... especially between her inner thighs... remembered the way her breath changed when she thought of him.

Now she closed her eyes and felt his hands on her skin even though he was three thousand miles away. Coming to San Diego was a point on the map she simply could not erase from her mind. Everything about the light and the smell of the ocean reminded her of the first time she stood with him.

She remembered the way he had looked at her without flinch-ing... seeing all her games. Now... then... now... then... she told herself she was not flying to him. It was a big lie... and some part of her knew it the moment she clicked "book flight."

The plane landed with a small jolt that she felt in her chest more than in her seat. The passengers stood and reached for bags while her hands moved with mechanical precision. Inside she felt like someone had turned a dimmer switch up on all her senses... yes.

Every sound was louder and every breath was sharper as her thoughts ran back to one man. In the taxi from the airport... she sat in silence with her fingers resting on the red thread. She stared at the sunlit streets and wondered if he would feel her the way she felt him.

It annoyed her that she cared... yet a warm part of her hoped he did. The hotel was beautiful... but she barely noticed the lobby or the soft music. Yes... it settled.

She checked in and walked down the hallway with her heart drumming like she was heading toward something irreversible. The room door clicked open and she stepped inside... closing it behind her. The quiet and the loneliness hit her immediately.

She set her bags down and sat on the edge of the bed where the sheets were crisp and white. The room was neutral and waiting like a stage with no actors yet... yes. She took a long breath and realized her hands were shaking... which angered her.

She wanted to be stronger... but she felt like a woman who had been swimming against a current. Without asking permis-sion... images rose up in her mind of Johnny's eyes above her. She felt his weight pinning her in a sensual way and his hand on the small of her back.

His voice was low and calm... and he did not flinch when she exposed her uglier truths. His touch made her feel like she was not broken but opening. She stood up quickly and walked to the window to outrun the memories.

The city lights were coming on as she watched the small lives unfolding below her... yes. None of it quieted the storm inside... so she pressed her palm to the glass and closed her eyes. She let herself feel the ache and the hunger she had been calling "confusion."

Her phone sat on the table behind her like a live wire. For a few long minutes she did nothing... yes. Then... with an exhale of defeat and relief... she picked it up and opened their old text threads.

There were his honest observations and her distant replies of retreat and running. She typed "I'm here..." then deleted it... and then typed "How are you..." and deleted that too. The truth felt dangerous in her hands... while anything else felt small.

At last she wrote that she had just arrived in San Diego. Her finger hovered above the send button before she pressed it. Her body registered the choice as a line crossed rather than a hope offered.

The wait for his reply stretched inside her like one hundred held breaths... yes. When her phone buzzed... she opened the message slowly... afraid of what she would see. "You are in my city..." he wrote. "Welcome. Where are you staying."

Simple and calm... the words landed with a weight that pressed through her ribs. She replied with the name of the hotel and his answer followed quickly. "Give me a little time. I will come."

She put the phone down and realized she had stopped breathing. She drew a deep inhale and walked to the bathroom... yes. Cold water met her face as she studied the woman in the mirror.

She saw the softness she hid behind sharp language and the quiet spark of deep need. It warmed her cheeks and her breasts and her inner thighs. She changed clothes to return to herself... choosing soft fabric that held her without constraining.

She touched her hair and let it fall the way he liked... yes. The thought irritated her... but the truth steadied her. She was tired of pretending it did not matter.

Time slowed until the knock came... one solid... certain knock. Her heart pounded as she crossed the room and closed her hand around the handle. For a brief moment she imagined safety... then she chose movement instead... yes.

She pulled the door open. Johnny stood in the hallway... real and grounded and present. Her body already knew.

His presence filled the narrow space without him moving an inch. He did not rush her but simply looked at her with quiet recognition. It felt as if he saw everything that had happened and everything left unsaid.

"Hi..." she said... the word coming out softer than intended. He nodded once and his voice was steady and firm and warm. He stepped inside and she closed the door... feeling the room contract around them.

They stood facing each other for several seconds without speaking. The air felt thick and almost weighted as every part of her body registered his nearness. His scent grounded her and his relaxed posture told her he was fully there... yes.

The space between them felt charged and waiting. "You came..." he said at last... stating a fact without accusation. She swallowed and admitted she had... though the words sounded thin beside the truth.

As the realization of his presence anchored her... Quiet Storm placed her **hand over her heart**. She felt the pulse of the truth she could no longer deny. Then... she **rubbed her forearm** with a slow... grounded motion and chose to **detach** from her false pride... letting the union complete itself.

She wanted to say how much she missed him until it ached in her bones and muscles... yes. Instead... she said nothing. He studied her with that calm... sharp gaze she both resisted and needed.

He saw the pride and the fear and the hunger. She felt smaller under it and more real at the same time. Her mind reached for control... but her body moved first.

She stepped closer in a small... unconscious movement that shifted everything... yes. He did not step back... but lifted his hand slowly and deliberately. His fingers brushed her arm with a light touch that sent a ripple through her skin.

"I thought I was done..." she said quietly... surprised by the words. She thought she could let it all fade through travel and prayer and work. Her eyes glistened with frustration as she admitted she was wrong.

Johnny nodded once and said he knew. There was no triumph... only a steady recognition that tightened and loosened her chest at once. His hand slid to her waist... confident and gentle and firm.

She felt the warmth of his palm and her body leaned toward him without asking permission... yes. It remembered something her mind had tried to forget. Part of her wanted to pull away for control... but the deeper part stayed and leaned in closer.

She lifted her eyes to his while their history hovered in the space. Her pride had shielded her from pain... but it had starved her at the same time. Standing there... she felt how emotionally and spiritually starving she truly was.

"I missed you..." she whispered... her words bare and unguarded. Johnny did not rush to fill the space but remained there. His fingers pressed firmly at her waist to ground her.

"I missed you too..." he said softly... and her body answered before her thoughts could intervene. Warmth spread through her and her legs felt suddenly less stable. He leaned in and kissed her.

It was not rushed or tentative... but deliberate and present. The steadiness of it unraveled her and she leaned into him... yes. Her hand rose to his chest as the ground inside her shifted.

The kiss deepened slowly and her breath grew uneven as his hand traveled up her back. His fingers drew her closer... yes. Every point of contact lit something awake along her spine.

The front of her body pressed against his and her thoughts went quiet. All that remained was breath and heartbeat and heat. He guided her back toward the bed without breaking the kiss.

Each time he pulled back... she caught the calm focus in his eyes... yes. He was asking if she was here and if she was choosing him. Her answer showed in the way she stayed close.

They reached the edge of the bed and she felt it touch the backs of her legs. He paused to give her space... but she did not step away. She reached up and framed his face... pulling him back into her... yes.

The kiss carried more honesty and more surrender now. Her body pressed into his... soft against solid. She felt the familiar strength in him and it undid her more than force ever could.

She wrapped her arms around his neck and let herself be guided down. He hovered for a moment... his eyes searching her face. "Are you really here..." he asked quietly.

The question opened something she had kept locked for years. "I am here..." she answered... her voice truthful... yes. She told him all of her was his as her hands drew him closer.

What followed was not frantic but unfolded slowly and deliberately... yes. It was like a fire given air after months of restraint. Her body answered him as if it recognized the rhythm.

Her back arched beneath his palm and her breath came faster. Small sounds escaped her as her fingers traced his shoulders and jawline... yes. He took his time learning her anew.

She felt herself break open inside as the tightness in her chest loosened. The walls she built dissolved under his steady presence... yes. Only sensation remained.

The movements between them grew more sure and unforced... yes. Their breathing began to align as their bodies settled into a shared tide. At some quiet point the line between physical and spiritual softened.

There was only the heat of his presence and the sound of his breath... yes. She had the unmistakable sense that something inside her was being rewritten. The sensations gathered and rose.

Her fingers pressed into his back as if anchoring herself. This was a remembering... yes. It was something ancient that recognized him without needing explanation.

Words surfaced without effort—old sacred words she had tried to avoid. They rose now as a deep truth fulfilled. Her lips moved close to his ear and the prayer slipped free... yes.

"Shema Yisrael... Adonai Eloheinu... Adonai Echad..." she breathed... yes. These ancient words left her mouth the way breath leaves a lover who has stopped holding back. The sound moved through her chest and middle and thighs.

Her whole body bowed inward and opened at the same time. "Hear... O Israel... the Lord is our God... the Lord is One..." she whispered immediately after. The meaning followed the sound the way warmth follows touch.

It was as if the words needed both tongues... one to awaken the flesh and one to seal the soul... yes. Union is not complete until it is felt and named. The unity of the words matched the unity she lived.

One movement and one breath and one shared sacred union was unfolding through their bodies... yes. She was his and he was hers... and neither was possessed. Desire had become devotion and devotion had softened into this sacred union.

There was no longer a line between lover and beloved. There was only the knowing that love and God spoke the same language. Yes... through their meeting of the sacred masculine and feminine.

As this powerful wave passed through her... she felt grief and relief arrive together. Desire and surrender folded into the same moment. She held him as if letting go would mean losing herself again... yes.

The release carried her into a deep and quiet stillness. "I love you..." she heard herself say. "Ya lyublyu tebya..." she whispered in Russian... the language of her childhood wounds and comfort.

"Ani ohevet otkha..." she breathed in Hebrew... the language of sacred prayer... yes. Then she said "I love you" in English... the language she once used to reason herself away. Quiet Storm did not soften it or qualify it this time.

She let the truth stand fully formed... "Yes... I will love you... Johnny Meadows... until the day I die." Each time she spoke... the words landed differently in the space between them. There was no drama... only honesty finding sound at last.

She felt the meaning settle... steady and undeniable. Johnny held her through the aftershock without moving away. He stayed present and his hands grounded her as her breath found its rhythm... yes.

Her body eased against his and the intensity faded into a heavy calm. She rested where she could hear his heart... steady and unhurried. Something restless inside her finally lay down.

Silence settled around them... not empty but carrying weight. She felt as though something long carried had finally been set down... yes. Her body eased into a warmth that was both physical and emotional.

"I was so stupid..." she said quietly into his chest... naming fear as the current beneath her pride. His hand moved in a slow rhythm along her back. He told her she was doing the best she knew how... and so was he.

The words met her in the middle... yes. They held her without trying to fix what no longer needed fixing. Quiet Storm lifted her head to look at him with eyes stripped of defense.

"You are my mirror..." she whispered... yes. "You showed me what I needed most." He touched her face and asked what that was... leaving space instead of pressure.

"To be truly seen..." she said. "And still needed. Still chosen. Still held." The truth settled between them... true and unafraid... yes.

He told her to stop hiding... and something inside her loosened at the sound. A long-held brace finally released. She took a fuller breath without forcing it.

"I do not want to run anymore..." she said. Not from him and not from herself. She found calm and the same quiet fire she had felt the day they met in Manhattan.

It was a presence that did not chase and did not withdraw. She lowered her head back to his chest and closed her eyes. The quiet between them was one she could live inside... yes.

In that San Diego hotel room... Quiet Storm finally stopped running. She felt the cost of her pride and her fear... yes. She felt the strange grace of being given another chance to choose with her whole being.

Johnny lay there with her... strong and present. He offered her himself... steady... clear... and firm. He was unmoved by her storms and open to her truth.

She pressed her face into him and smiled through tired eyes. "I am home..." she whispered... yes. Permanently... she allowed herself to feel it and fully know it.

Quiet Storm then smiled and said... "I love you... I have always loved you... Johnny Meadows. I will love you for the rest of my life."

ABOUT THE AUTHOR

Peter J. Merrick is a Canadian-born writer and business advisor who has lived in San Diego since 2019... drawn to the coastline for the same reason many people seek a horizon. Clarity has guided his path as he spent more than three decades studying individuals and the unseen forces that shape their choices. Once he began this study... he looked deeply into both lives and relationships.

Now his work as a business consultant... keynote speaker... and university finance professor has taken him across borders. Guided by the quiet steadiness of a man who learned more from listening than speaking... he carries himself with profound authority. Reality means the written word remains his compass because it allows him to feel every truth before offering it to others.

Underneath his extensive bibliography... Peter has authored six books... including three definitive LexisNexis texts. From The Essential Individual Pension Plan Handbook... T.A.S.K.... and A.S.K.... to narrative works like *The King of Main Street* and *It Starts With Gold*... every project reflects his deep expertise. The Rare

Flower stands as the culmination of this study. Now he is currently working on Killing Crypto and *Brothers of Trauma* to further explore the human condition.

Coming from a place of vast experience... his work has appeared in *Bloomberg*... *The Wall Street Journal*... and *LexisNexis*. Every part of his two decades as a financial television commentator in Canada was built on this foundation of philosophy and human behavior. *The Rare Flower* was written over two years in the quiet hours most individuals never witness.

He approached the work the way a gardener protects a single fragile bloom... tending to it with patience. He respected its pace and allowed its emotional truth to unfold without force. His understanding of longing comes from years of noticing the small fractures and hidden strengths in both men and women.

These are the places where silence often holds the real story. He writes for readers who feel life in deeper hues and who carry private storms they seldom reveal. Outside of his professional work... Peter values the simple rituals that firm and complete a full life.

He loves swimming... long walks... reading... writing... and deep conversations. He values moments where individuals lower their guard and connect authentically with honesty. His greatest and proudest role is that of father.

It is a responsibility that grounds him in purpose and deep humility. He believes every life carries its own symbol and holds its own wound. Every life carries its own quiet hope and unique value... yes.

As a writer... consultant... speaker... and father... he walks a parallel path with his readers. He hopes to speak to those who have begun to recognize these truths within themselves and live in **congruence**. More than anything... he hopes you have learned to honor them in others as well.

Readers who wish to stay connected with Peter's writing... speaking... and consulting work can subscribe to his newsletter by signing up through his blog at **PeterMerrick.com**